HILDA THE BRITON

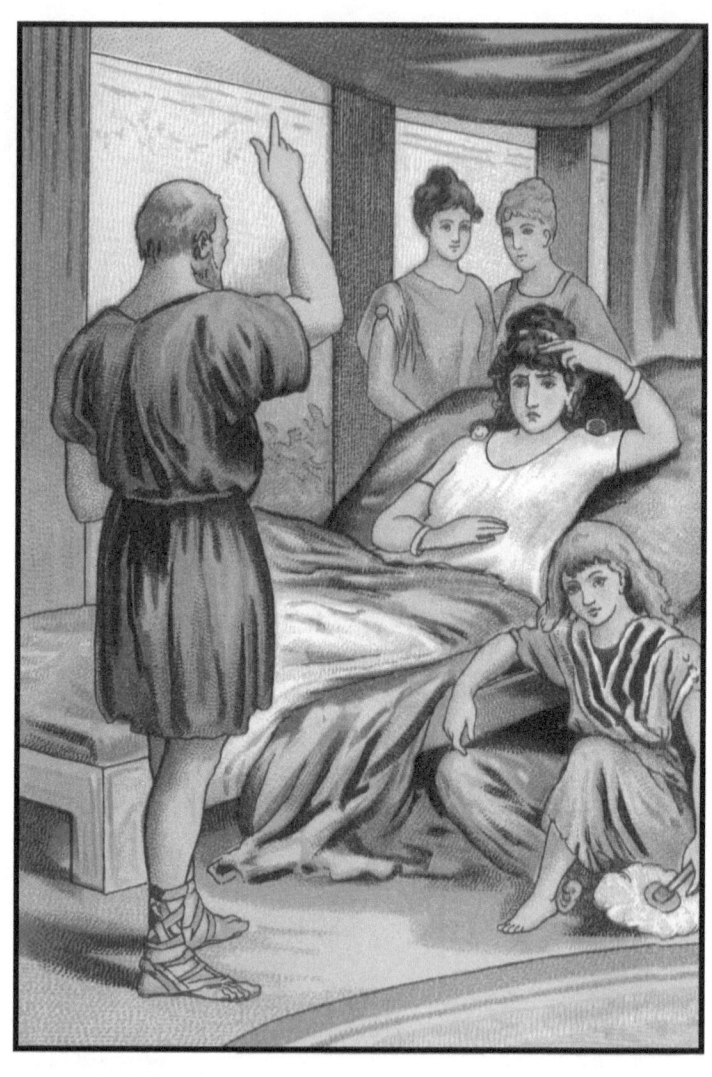

ANICETUS BEGAN THE WONDROUS STORY.

Page 74

EMMA LESLIE
JUNIOR CHURCH HISTORY SERIES

HILDA THE BRITON

OR,

THE GOLDEN AGE

THE STORY OF A ROMAN SLAVE GIRL

BY

EMMA LESLIE

Illustrated by
BUTTERWORTH & HEATH

A symbol of the early Church containing
the first letter for each word in the Greek phrase
Jesus Christ, Son of God, Savior

Salem Ridge Press
Emmaus, Pennsylvania

Originally Published
1874
The Religious Tract Society

Republished 2010
Salem Ridge Press LLC
4263 Salem Drive
Emmaus, Pennsylvania 18049

www.salemridgepress.com

Hardcover ISBN: 978-1-934671-36-8
Softcover   ISBN: 978-1-934671-37-5

PUBLISHER'S NOTE

Although not a very long story, *Hilda the Briton* contains several valuable lessons for its readers. Hilda's fellow slaves wait for their masters to do the right thing and set the example, while she demonstrates a willingness to be the first one to do what is right. Also, Hilda chooses to obey God's commands even though she has no idea what the results will be.

Through Hilda's example, we are reminded that we should be willing to do what is right regardless of the outcome and regardless of the choices that others are making. I hope that this story will be an encouragement to each one of us to do just that.

Daniel Mills

April, 2010

HISTORICAL NOTES

In 55 B.C. Julius Cæsar led the first Roman invasion of the island of Britain. He did very little conquering but convinced many of the tribes to pay tribute to him in exchange for peace. Over the next several decades, Rome supported the local kings and queens as they ruled their own fiercely independent tribes. Although several invasions were planned, a full-scale Roman invasion of Britain did not come until almost one hundred years later.

In A.D. 43, Roman forces led by General Aulus Plautius conquered southern Britain. Soon after this, the Roman city of Londinium (London) was established. Then, in A.D. 60, a few years before *Hilda the Briton* takes place, British Queen Boudica rebelled against the Romans. She attacked and destroyed several cities, including Londinium. The Roman army retaliated and in a decisive battle, killed tens of thousands of Boudica's warriors.

HISTORICAL NOTES

Over the next few centuries, the Romans continued to expand their territory but their efforts were often hampered by Britain's distance from Rome and political unrest throughout the Empire. By the fifth century the weakened Roman Empire was no longer able to maintain control of Britain, opening the way for invasion by the Saxon peoples from northern Germany.

Each year, in late December, the Romans held a week-long celebration called the **Saturnalia**, named after their god Saturn. During the Saturnalia all of the slaves in Rome were allowed to pretend that they were free. They were also released from many of their normal duties.

Two of the minor characters in *Hilda the Briton* are based on a quote from Paul in his second letter to Timothy which reads:

HISTORICAL NOTES

Do thy diligence to come before winter. Eubulus greeteth thee, and Pudens, *and Linus, and* Claudia, *and all the brethren.*

II Timothy 4:21

Scholars, including Archbishop James Usshur, author of *The Annals of the World* in the 17th century, have associated the Claudia listed in *II Timothy* with Claudia Rufina, a British princess in the first century who was the wife of Roman centurion Aulus Pudens. It is not known for sure if this is the case.

CONTENTS

ILLUSTRATIONS

HILDA THE BRITON

Hilda the Briton

Chapter I

The British Slaves

THE sun was drawing near the western horizon, brightening with its last declining rays the patches of heath and gorse that grew so plentifully along the edges of the great Roman road leading from London to the seacoast. Along this road tramped a weary crowd of captives, men and women, boys and girls, being chained to each other by the wrist or ankle like animals; as animals, indeed, their Roman masters looked upon them. They were a party of Britons on

HEATH AND GORSE: *small shrubs*

their way to the slave-market of Rome. Despair was written on every face in that little company, except the youngest, a fair-haired, blue-eyed girl of twelve; she was trying to raise the drooping spirits of her brother, who was walking beside her, but whose ankles and wrists were bleeding from the chains that dragged at them. Her limbs were left free, for her captors knew that in securing her brother they had taken little Hilda's sole remaining relative; and she loved her brother so dearly that there was little fear of her trying to escape, even if they had not been marching through a part of the country quite unknown to her.

She looked round at the wide stretch of bleak, bare heath, and then forward at the steep hill they would presently have to climb, for these Roman roads always went straight on over the hills that lay in their way, seldom winding round to avoid the steepness or lessen the labor of those who

LIMBS: *arms and legs*

had to travel by them. She was weary, and her legs ached with her long march; but she disdained to shed a tear, for her mother had taught her that it was a disgrace for a British maiden to cry for pain or weariness. So little Hilda trudged on without a word of complaint.

At length she broke the silence by saying, "Bran, will our forest spirits help us when we get to Rome?"

"I don't believe our forest spirits can help us, Hilda," said the boy, bitterly looking down at the chains on his wrists.

"And they won't be angry with us again?" said the little girl, in a timid whisper.

"They can't do us any more harm if they are angry," answered Bran; "for nothing can be worse than slavery."

Hilda knew they were prisoners, but she did not understand what slavery was, and presently she said, "I wish somebody would help me up this hill; I am so tired."

Bran looked at the pale, weary face, and then at the chains on his hands, but he only said, "Be brave, Hilda, and walk a little farther; we shall rest soon, I am sure."

But another mile had to be traveled before the Roman guard gave the signal for a halt, and the prisoners were allowed to throw themselves upon the ground to rest for the night. There was little fear that these weary captives would try to escape, for their spirits were too crushed and broken by recent disaster and defeat; but sentinels were set to watch them, and at the earliest dawn of day they were roused and on the road again. At length this weary march came to an end, for a time at least, for the seashore was reached, and they embarked on board the Roman galley that was to take them to the opposite coast of Gaul, where another band of soldiers would take charge of them; and after a day or two they would set forward with other prisoners on the long march to Rome.

EMBARKED ON BOARD: *boarded*
GALLEY: *a ship propelled by oars*
GAUL: *the Roman name for France*

What a weary march this was! Hilda thought it would never come to an end; and in spite of all her resolutions not to distress Bran she could not help shedding tears very often, for her feet were blistered and sore, and she began to fear that the forest spirits, of whom she had lived in such dread all her life, were very angry with her and her brother, or they would not have let the soldiers carry them away from their beloved land of Britain. She longed to reach Rome, but Bran dreaded it, for hard as his lot now was, it might be worse there; so he only shook his head despairingly when Hilda spoke of what she overheard concerning the riches and grandeur of the imperial city.

The weary march was almost over at last, and in the distance they could see the marble palaces and splendid temples of the great city. A feeling of awe crept over Hilda as she looked at these wonderful buildings, and drawing nearer to her brother she

IMPERIAL CITY: *capital city of the empire*

whispered, "These Romans worship a god they call Jupiter; he must be greater than our gods, and his priests wiser than our Druids. Shall we worship Jupiter by-and-by?"

Bran shook his head. "Every nation has its own gods," he said.

"But ours—where are they?" asked Hilda; "If they stay in Britain, shall we have to do without a god here in Rome?"

"We shall not be worse off than if we were in Britain, seeing our gods have forsaken us," replied Bran.

They were drawing near the gates of the grand old city, and the poor, dirty, half-clad Britons who ventured to raise their eyes could not but wonder why it was that a people possessed of so much wealth should come to rob them of their woods and plains, their simple food of roots and acorns, and carry them away as slaves. This last thought was the bitterest of all to the proud-spirited, independent people, and they scarcely noticed

JUPITER: *the ruler of all the gods in Roman mythology*

the gaily decorated chariots or the splendid robes of the people who brushed against them as they passed.

They were to be taken at once to the slave-market and sold, so they were soon transferred from the soldiers to a regular dealer, who drove them like a flock of sheep to the lower part of the town, where the poorer part of the people lived, and near which was the market for the sale of Jews and Greeks, Egyptians and Britons, for all the captive nations were taxed to supply the luxurious Romans with their numerous slaves.

Bran and Hilda were placed together, their owner hoping he should be able to dispose of them to the same purchaser; not because he was unwilling to separate the brother and sister, but because he thought a better bargain could be made by this arrangement, for Bran, though strong and tall for his age, looked sullen and defiant—more especially if Hilda was out of his sight for a moment—

and this would greatly lessen his value if it were noticed. Hilda, however, with her delicate face and fair hair, was far more prepossessing in appearance, and might bring a good price if she did not spoil her looks by fretting, which she would be sure to do if parted from her brother. And so their owner refused several times to separate them when asked to do so—a fact not unnoticed by Bran, who had learned to understand a little of the Latin language from the soldiers who had brought them from Britain.

The thought of being separated from his little sister had not crossed his mind before; they were slaves, he knew, but they would be sold together, of course, for no one would think of taking one without the other. This was what he had thought, if he had thought at all upon the matter, and his face grew fierce and dark in its anger when he heard someone propose to purchase Hilda without himself.

PREPOSSESSING: *favorable*

IN THE SLAVE MARKET

Happily, however, there came a customer at length who wanted two such slaves as Hilda and Bran; and the bargain was quickly concluded, the only stipulation being that the brother and sister should each have a bath—for they were very dirty—and throw away the filthy rags of clothing they now wore. This innovation Bran resisted at first, but Hilda submitted to it without demur, and felt rather pleased with the white linen tunic that was given to her instead of the coarse, dirty woollen blanket she had hitherto worn.

Before leaving the market they heard that the household to which they were going already numbered three hundred slaves; and Bran wondered what employment could be found for Hilda and himself among such a numerous train. Little Hilda, too, began to question what her work would be in this great household. "I can only watch the sheep and

STIPULATION: *condition*
INNOVATION: *new idea*
DEMUR: *objection*
TRAIN: *group of attendants*

milk the cows, Bran," she said in a troubled whisper, as they were on their way to their new home.

"I am afraid there will be no sheep or cows where we are going," said Bran, looking up at the stately houses by which they were surrounded.

"No sheep or cows!" said Hilda, who could not imagine a state of existence without these animals being in constant use.

They were still more bewildered when, on entering the vestibule of their master's dwelling, they saw a crowd of men and women passing through with a basket or pitcher on their heads, while in front stood a splendid chariot adorned with gold and silver.

"The noble Plautius cannot see you or your miserable British slaves either," said the porter, as the man who had taken them pushed his way in.

"*My* miserable British slaves!" repeated

VESTIBULE: *entrance hall*
PORTER: *doorkeeper*
NICHE: *alcove*

the man, with a short laugh; "they are your master's, not mine; your companions, my fine popinjay," he added, contemptuously; and without another word he walked away, leaving Bran and Hilda in the middle of the vestibule, and the angry porter looking at them with a frown.

"You must stand out of the way," he said at last, pushing them into a niche; "my master is going to the Forum this morning, and cannot be hindered to look at you." And the next minute the heavy silken curtain that divided the *atrium* from the vestibule was drawn aside by the attendant slave, and the noble Roman, in a long flowing robe, came slowly forward.

Bran recognized him in a moment, and the patrician paused as his eyes fell on his new purchases. "Take them to the slaves' quarters, and give them something to eat," he said, turning to one of the attendants as he passed on.

FORUM: *the central meeting place and court of Rome*
ATRIUM: *the central room in a Roman house*
PATRICIAN: *member of the upper class in ancient Rome*

Bran looked round on his new companions, who were assembled in a paved courtyard, some idly lounging on the ground, others engaged in a game of chance, while a few were preparing vegetables for cooking, and food for the lampreys in the adjacent fish-pond. They raised their eyes as Bran and Hilda came in, and there was a contemptuous shrug of the shoulders as the words went from lip to lip, "Savage Britons."

One old man, however, seemed to pity their strange, forlorn condition, and came forward to speak to them. "You are Britons," he said, "and only lately arrived in Rome?"

Bran nodded. "I was never a slave before," he said, impatiently.

"A slave's condition is not so bad if he has a good master," said the old man, soothingly.

But Bran shook his head. "Slaves are ever to be despised," he said; and he looked down pityingly at his little sister, who held his hand more closely than ever.

LAMPREYS: *thin eel-like fish*

The old man noticed the look. "That is your little sister?" he said questioningly. "The Lord has been merciful to you both, that you are sold together."

"The Lord!" repeated Bran; "do you mean the man who bought us?"

"Nay; but the Lord God Almighty, who made heaven and earth. He has taken care of you, my children," added the old man, gently.

But Bran only looked indifferent. "I don't believe in any god now," he said. "Your gods of Rome may be all very well for you, as they have conquered our gods, and made us your slaves; but there is no god for us now;" and he turned away to look at the game of hazard being played close by.

Hilda, who only half understood what had been said, felt sorry for the old man when she saw the look of disappointment on his face as he turned away, and resolved to speak to him by-and-by if she had the

HAZARD: *dice*

opportunity. Bran was anxious to discover what his work in this strange household was likely to be, and what employment could be found for a little girl like Hilda. The latter question was soon answered, for an elderly slave woman came to fetch her about half an hour afterwards, for she was to begin learning the duties of a lady's-maid at once, and one of these was to know how to mix the goat's milk, honey, and oatmeal used for the daily bath.

Bran was told what his sister's work was to be, and he felt thankful that it was not very hard and laborious; for the young lady who was to be her mistress already had some half-dozen slaves to wait upon her and prepare her perfumes and unguents, and he encouraged Hilda to be patient and brave, as she went away to another part of the house.

Poor little Hilda felt very lonely in this large, strange house, where everybody spoke

UNGUENTS: *ointments*

the Roman language, and dressed in a fashion that was quite new to her. She was filled with awe, too, at the sight of the statues of gods and goddesses that everywhere surrounded her, and felt half afraid when left alone beside a marble Flora in the *atrium*, lest the goddess should descend from her flower-wreathed pedestal, and drive her out of the beautiful hall. She was still more dazzled when the curtain was drawn aside, and she was taken into the next room, or marble-paved hall—the *peristyle*, this was called. A silken curtain was drawn over the center, which formed the ceiling, while round it was a colonnade of graceful marble pillars, supporting a gallery above, between which hung baskets of the rarest and sweetest flowers. Under the gallery were ranged tables and couches. On one of these sat two ladies, very elegantly dressed, the younger of whom looked very cross, and the other very unhappy.

FLORA: *the Roman goddess of flowers and spring*
COLONNADE: *row*
GALLERY: *balcony*

"Oh, this is my new slave," said the young lady, after Hilda had been brought in. "What do you think of her, Mother?" she asked.

The elder lady only shook her head, mournfully. "I dare say Felicita can make her useful," she said, with a deep sigh.

"She *must* make her useful, or I will have them both beaten," said the young lady, glancing at her older slave as she spoke. She still stood with drooping head and downcast eyes near the entrance, waiting for her mistress to conclude her examination of this new acquisition.

"Come here, girl, and tell me what you can do," said the lady.

But poor Hilda could only stare and look half frightened, for she did not understand what was said, and therefore did not venture any closer to the ladies.

Felicita explained this to her mistress, but the lady was very angry: "A little savage Briton, who does not understand a word that

ACQUISITION: *purchase*

is said. Send her back to the slave-market; she is of no use."

"But we shall have to keep her, since your father has bought her," said the elder lady, languidly.

"Then Felicita must teach her our language, and she must learn it quickly, or I will not have her;" and stamping her foot impatiently, the lady motioned to Felicita to take her away.

Bran was summoned to give his sister her first lesson in the language of their masters, and Hilda very soon learned all he could teach her; but from this as a beginning it was not so difficult to make her understand all that was necessary at present, and then she began the compounding of unguents, spices, and perfumes, under Felicita's direction.

Meanwhile, Bran had quarrelled with several of his fellow-slaves, and positively refused to do some of the tasks imposed upon

LANGUIDLY: *without interest*
COMPOUNDING: *mixing*

him. The latter, however, was only known to the old man who had spoken to him on his first arrival, and who had done the work himself rather than expose Bran to the punishment he knew would follow such daring disobedience.

Poor Bran! his work was not at all agreeable to him, for he had been set to help the cook in preparing vegetables, fruit, and poultry, work that he looked upon as only fit for girls and women. If it had only been work in the fields it would not have been so irksome to the strong, active young Briton; but to be kept within four walls, often standing or sitting still all day, was worse than the most laborious work to him, and he chafed, and fretted, and grumbled, until everyone began to look upon him as a dissatisfied, ill-tempered fellow, whom no one cared to please or help even when they were able to do it.

But, although everybody else shunned poor Bran, his old friend still remained

IRKSOME: *tiresome*
CHAFED: *was annoyed*

faithful, and frequently showed him some little kindness, although he was rarely thanked for it. But for Hilda it seemed as though Bran could not have lived through this misery. He often saw his little sister, for Felicita would send her on various errands about the house, and sometimes she would stop and pluck a few feathers from the bird Bran was preparing for the spit or oven.

During these visits their old friend, Anicetus, often spoke to her, telling her about the wonderful River Tiber that was covered with ships from all parts of the world, and the beautiful valleys that were beyond the city gates, where grapes and figs grew in rich profusion. He promised to take her to see the river and the valley when the Saturnalia came round, but Bran shook his head as he heard the promise given, for it was never likely to be fulfilled, he thought. He did not know that every year when the month of December came round there was a feast to the god Saturn, when everybody

SATURN: *the Roman god of farming*

in Rome, old and young, rich and poor, had such a holiday that even the slaves did as they pleased—went out or stayed at home, feasted and made merry just as they liked. Hilda was told of this great holiday, and began to look forward to it; but Bran only smiled grimly when she asked what they should do and where they should go when the Saturnalia came.

Chapter II

The Strange Prisoner

THE Saturnalia came at last, and every slave in Rome was at liberty to please himself, for a few days at least, and the city seemed to have gone crazy with rollicking mirth. All the streets were lined with booths, where little grotesque figures of satyrs, beings supposed to be half men and half goats, were sold. Children in white linen dresses, with gilt balls hung round their necks, crowded to these; while the merry, mocking crowd of slaves and nobles, Romans, Greeks, Britons, and Germans, pushed and jostled each other, some on their way to the amphitheatre to see the gladiators fight, and some

ROLLICKING MIRTH: *carefree laughter*
GILT: *gold-colored*

on their way to visit friends, or join the fun. Here and there a more quiet group might be seen making their way towards the barracks of the Prætorian guard, and among these was the old slave, leading the little British girl Hilda.

She, too, had a gilt ball hung round her neck, and a little satyr in her hand, and she was telling Anicetus what Felicita had told her of the meaning of this Saturnalia.

"It must have been a good glad time to live in, when Father Saturn reigned over the earth and heaven, and there were no quarrels between the gods or men," said little Hilda, repeating almost word for word the story she had been told.

Anicetus looked down on the little girl. "Do you like to hear stories?" he asked.

"I like to hear Felicita tell of Father Saturn," she said; "are we going to his temple?"

The old man shook his head. "You shall hear of a better god than Saturn," he said.

PRÆTORIAN GUARD: *the bodyguards of the Emperor*

"Bran says there cannot be a better god, since he kept the rest from quarrelling; for if the gods had not quarrelled, and our forest spirits had not been conquered by Jupiter, your Roman god, we should not be slaves."

"Nay, but it was our Roman swords and brave soldiers who conquered Britain; Jupiter could not fight a battle," said Anicetus.

"I thought it was your gods who helped you," said Hilda, wonderingly; and then she added, "Saturn shall be my god, Anicetus; I like him better than Flora, although she is good and kind, and gives us all the flowers."

"And why do you like Saturn best, little one?" asked the old man.

"Because he makes the corn to grow—it used to grow without being planted, Felicita says; and then he is kind to all alike, slaves as well as nobles, and that is why all are equal now, and Bran may wear the freedman's cap and hide the holes in his ears. I have prayed to Father Saturn," went on Hilda; "I have

CORN: *wheat*

asked him to help us, and bring the golden age again, when everybody will be kind, and the gods will not quarrel."

"It is men's quarrels that make the misery, Hilda; men and women and boys and girls being cruel and unkind to each other. The gods have nothing to do with this."

Hilda sighed. "But if the gods had not quarrelled the Romans would not have come to conquer our Britain," she said.

This was Bran's view of the matter, and she stoutly maintained whatever her brother said.

Other quiet, orderly groups had entered the same street, and kindly greetings were exchanged between Anicetus and many of these; but the old man still held Hilda's hand, until they reached a house at the door of which stood a soldier, who greeted Anicetus as if he had been an old friend.

The little girl was more surprised than ever at this, for she had been long enough at Rome to understand that the soldiers were very proud and quite despised the slaves, and that Anicetus should be allowed to enter the house unquestioned was to her very strange. More strange still was the sight that awaited her in the large bare hall or *atrium* beyond. Here a number of people were gathered; noble ladies in costly dresses, and humble slaves like herself and Anicetus, busy merchants, who could rarely have a holiday, and rough-looking soldiers, who gained their living by plunder and robbery. They were gathered round an old man who sat in the middle, chained by the wrist to a soldier. Someone was speaking when they entered, and Hilda soon found that it was the prisoner, but she was too much occupied in looking about her to listen to what was said until Anicetus stooped and whispered, "Listen, little one, for this prisoner Paul is the messenger of the great God of heaven."

"Is he as great and kind as Saturn?" asked Hilda, half aloud.

As if answering the little girl's question, the prisoner raised his unchained hand at this moment and said, "My brethren, I come to tell you of One in whose sight all are equal, slave or noble, One who loves and pities you, and would make you joyful and happy, not with the noisy folly and hollow joy of this Saturnalia, which often brings sorrow to the heart afterwards, but true joy and true happiness, even rest and peace in His love."

"It is about Father Saturn," whispered Hilda.

But Anicetus shook his head, "Listen, little one," he said.

"This Lord God Almighty, who made heaven and earth, made man to dwell here in holiness and happiness. There was no sin or sorrow, no blighting of flowers, no death or pain. But man soon rebelled against God, disobeyed His commands, and this was the

BLIGHTING: *withering*

THE STRANGE TEACHER

beginning of sin and misery; from this came wars, and fighting, and pain, and death. And there was but one remedy, one cure for all this sorrow and suffering; God's Son, the Lord Jesus Christ, came into this world as a man, and tasted pain and sickness, sorrow and death, that man might be redeemed from the power of death and sin, for He alone was without sin. And this is the good news of the gospel I have to tell you today, that 'Jesus Christ came into world to save sinners,'[1] came to bear our sins and carry our sorrows, and make us fit to live with Him in holiness and happiness beyond the grave." This was not all that was said, but all that Hilda could remember, and she resolved not to forget it, but to tell her brother the good news she had heard, and, if possible, persuade him to come and hear it for himself.

As they were returning towards home, she suddenly asked Anicetus if he had heard of this great God before.

[1] I TIMOTHY 1:15

"Yes, little one, I learned it from the lips of our great teacher Paul when he first came to Rome, almost a year since," answered the old man.

"And has Felicita heard about Him too; did she make a mistake when she called Him Saturn?" asked the child.

"No, I am afraid Felicita has never heard this good news, and she still believes in the vain idols that are called gods, although they are but images of gold or marble, like the Flora standing in the garden at home."

"Flora only marble!" exclaimed Hilda, for she had been told that it was through the power of this goddess that the flowers grew, and put on all the beautiful colors and shed forth such sweet perfume.

"Yes; the image that is decked with flowers has no more power to make them grow than the stone of this pavement on which we are walking," said the old man.

Hilda looked doubtful. "Who does make them grow?" she asked.

"The Lord God Almighty," said Anicetus, reverently.

"But you said He took care of men and women, and boys and girls," she replied, quickly.

"Yes; He takes care of us, and makes the corn and fruit and flowers grow for us," said her friend. "'Not a sparrow falls to the ground without Him.'"[1]

"Then if He does all this, what is there for the other gods to do? There are a great many gods besides Flora, you know."

"Yes, but they are all as helpless as the marble image you call Flora, for there is only one God, the Lord of heaven and earth, of whom Paul has told us today. These idols are but foolish fancies. When man sinned against God, he tried to hide himself, because he was ashamed, and to forget Him, as though that were enough to

[1] MATTHEW 10:29

take away his sin, and at last he had so far forgotten Him that he no longer knew His name, and so he grew to imagine that there must be different gods to perform the works of nature; one to make the flowers blossom, another to make the corn grow, and so each had a different work to do in the world, and the one true God was entirely forgotten, and men built temples to these vain idols, and burnt incense before their images."

Again Hilda sighed. "Then there never was a golden age when Saturn reigned, and it was always a holiday for slaves, and there never will be," said Hilda, a little discontentedly.

"There was a golden time before men sinned, when God came down and talked to Adam, but that is long, long ago," said Anicetus.

"And it will never come back again, I suppose?"

"No, that time can never come again; but God has prepared something better for those who love Him—a golden age when we shall see Him face to face, and never know sin or sorrow," said the old man, joyfully.

Hilda looked up into his face. "Will you be a slave then?" she asked.

"No; there are no slaves in the kingdom of heaven where God reigns."

"The kingdom of heaven where God reigns!" repeated Hilda. "Do they let little girls go into that kingdom?"

"Yes; the Lord Jesus Christ, God's own Son, has invited little children. He said, 'Suffer the little children to come unto Me, and forbid them not, for of such is the kingdom of heaven.'"[1]

"Then I'll go. Will you take me now?" said Hilda, promptly.

Anicetus looked puzzled, as the little hand clasped his own more tightly.

[1] MARK 10:14

"My little one, we must wait for this golden age, this kingdom of heaven; wait and work for God."

Little Hilda's eyes slowly filled with tears. "The golden ages are a long way off;" she said, "and I never heard of your God until today."

"But you will try to learn more about Him now that you have heard how much He loves you?" said Anicetus.

"Loves me! what does love mean?" asked the little girl, curiously, for in her fierce, cruel native land this word was hardly known, and Bran was half ashamed of the love he felt for his little sister, as though it were a weakness to be despised.

The old man knew this, and was perplexed as to the answer he should give, but at length he said, "You are pleased to help Bran when you have time, and he is glad to have you come, and is kind and gentle with you, although he may be cross with everybody else."

"Dear Bran, he is my brother!" exclaimed Hilda; "I wish I could always be with and help him."

"That is because you love him. This great God is your Father, and loves you more than you love Bran; and is often saying, 'Dear little Hilda, the slave in Rome, I love her, although she does not know it yet.' It was He who took care of you on the long journey from Britain, and made the man wish to sell you and Bran together; and by-and-by He will teach you to love Him too."

Hilda was staring at him incredulously. "I never saw this great God you are talking about," she said, a little impatiently.

"But He has seen you, is looking at you now, for He can see us at all times, and knows what we say and do."

The little girl looked round half frightened, half amazed. "It is worse than our forest spirits," she said, "for they only hear us when we are in the woods or near the sacred groves."

"Nay, nay, little one; thou must not be frightened because God is near at hand, and not afar off, for He is near to protect, and guide, and bless us."

But Hilda did not seem to be reassured until she was made to understand that God's love was as tender and pitiful as her brother's, and that He, unlike the dreaded forest spirits of her native land, delighted in showing kindness and mercy, instead of being cruel and revengeful.

When they reached home she went in search of her brother, to tell him of the strange things she had heard and seen, but Bran did not care to listen to her story just now. Dressed in the freedman's cap, he was trying to forget his slavery and believe he was free—free to drink wine and live riotously for a few days. Many besides were doing the same thing, so Bran was not alone in his folly, although he felt half ashamed of himself; as well as of his companions, when

PITIFUL: *compassionate*

he saw Hilda coming towards them, eager to tell of the golden age that was yet to come.

"The silly child has been listening to old Anicetus," said one.

"He goes to hear a story they call the gospel from one Paul, a prisoner," said another.

"Yes; and the old dotard believes that this gospel is to bring the golden age, will overturn the temples of Jupiter and Mars, and teach all men to love one another," put in a third.

This seemed so ridiculous to the rest that a loud laugh followed this speech, and one of them turning to Bran, said derisively, "Perhaps this gospel will find its way to your native Britain, and teach the savages to love one another."

Bran clenched his fist angrily at what seemed like an insult. "Britons may he savages," he said, "but they are brave and warlike, and will have nothing of this love message. Go away, Hilda," he said, seeing

OLD DOTARD: *foolish old man*
DERISIVELY: *mockingly*

the child was still standing near, and then turning towards the one who had suggested that the message of the gospel might be sent to his native land, he struck him in the face. The blow was quickly returned, and the fight might have become general had not an older slave interfered and separated the combatants. The rest wisely gave in at once; but poor foolish Bran turned and struck the intruder, who was a man of some authority in the household, although a slave, and the story of this having reached the master's ears he ordered him to be locked up in prison until the Saturnalia was over. In vain Anicetus pleaded that Bran was a stranger, and that it was the time of universal liberty; Plautius would not remit his punishment. "Slaves must not forget all law," he said; and so while the rest were enjoying themselves Bran was groaning the time away in his miserable stone cell.

REMIT HIS PUNISHMENT: *release him from his punishment*

Hilda had run away frightened when the slaves began fighting; but she heard of her brother's imprisonment early the next morning, and begged Anicetus to take her to him.

But the kind-hearted old man did not like the thought of her sharing her brother's punishment, as she wished. He deserved to suffer for his violence and anger, but it seemed cruel to shut up poor Hilda in that gloomy prison. There was also another reason why he was unwilling to do this; he wanted to take her with him to hear the preaching of Paul again, and when this universal holiday was over he might not have another opportunity, and he told Hilda of this. But still the little girl persisted in her request to be allowed to spend her holiday with her brother in prison, until at last Anicetus yielded to her request, and the long-anticipated Saturnalia was clouded for the old man as well as for Hilda and Bran.

CHAPTER III

A SAD HOLIDAY

HILDA remembered the words she had heard from Paul about sorrow often following the folly and mirth of this Saturnalia when she entered her brother's gloomy prison, and saw him crouching in the corner in misery and despair. At first he would not lift his head even to speak to her; but after a few minutes the little girl succeeded in slipping her arms round his neck, and laying her tearful face against his.

"Poor Bran! I am so sorry," she whispered; "but you must not cry; I will stop with you and tell you all about the golden age

STOP: *visit*

that is coming, when there will be a long holiday for poor slaves—a holiday that will last for ever and ever, and that won't make them sorry either."

"I don't want to hear about any golden age; there is nothing but misery anywhere for the poor," said Bran.

"But I want to tell you what I heard yesterday about a better God than Saturn; one who is greater than Jupiter and kinder than Flora."

"I don't want to hear anything about Roman gods," interrupted Bran.

"But the Lord God Almighty is not a Roman god; He is everybody's God, Anicetus says, and so He is just the God for us, because our forest spirits will not leave Britain," said Hilda, and she laid her head on her brother's shoulder, and smoothed the rough, tumbled hair so that the holes in his ears were completely concealed. "There, now you look like my British Bran," said Hilda, playfully, trying to make her brother smile.

But his heart was too heavy this morning; he had been thinking of all his hardships and wrongs until he felt angry with every-body—everybody but Hilda, and of his love for her he felt half ashamed, although it was the greatest comfort of his life. Now, while she played with his hair, he felt that the evil, angry spirit was leaving him, and a half wish that he could keep her with him always arose in his mind.

"If we could only be together I should not get so fierce and angry as I did yesterday," said Bran, after a pause.

Hilda opened her eyes. "Why not?" she said.

"Because I am never angry with you; I sup-pose that is it," answered Bran.

"Anicetus says we love each other, that is why you are kind, and never hurt me, and that this great God loves me just as much as you do."

Bran was at first inclined to feel angrily jealous, and to dispute this fact; but, looking at the fair young face now turned towards him so earnestly and wistfully, he thought it was not so wonderful, and he said, "Well, suppose He does, Hilda; will you want to go away from me?"

"Oh no; I shall never go away from you. But, Bran, if it is true that this God takes care of us, and made the man sell us together, and does so much for us, we ought to love Him, because I love you for loving me."

Bran smiled at this reasoning, but it amused him to hear her talk now, and so he said, "Tell me all you heard about this new God yesterday."

"He is not a new God, but the very oldest of all. Anicetus says that Saturn and Jupiter are not gods at all, that there is but One, the Lord Almighty, and He does everything for us, and everything in the world. He made

WONDERFUL: *surprising*

the first man, and that was the golden age, because there was no quarrelling or fighting, and no slaves; but then came sin and—"

"But what is sin?" asked Bran, who had never heard the word before.

"Rebellion, Anicetus says; doing what this great God says we are not to do."

"And what does He say we are not to do?" asked Bran, curiously.

"We are not to be unkind to anybody, but love Him because He loves us."

"And you went to this strange God's temple yesterday?" asked Bran, who had now become quite interested.

"He has not got a temple in Rome yet," replied Hilda; "but He has sent His messenger, Paul, with the good news that there is another golden age coming, better than this Saturnalia, even if it could last always."

"Another golden age better than the Romans tell of when their god Saturn shall rule the world?" exclaimed Bran.

"Yes; and this God loves all people, the poor slaves and the rich nobles alike," said Hilda; and then she went on to tell him of the kingdom Anicetus had spoken of, where there were no slaves, no sin, no death or pain.

"Hilda, if this story were only true, it would be good news for the whole world; but it can't be true," said Bran, sadly; "it is too good to be true."

"But Anicetus says that it is; that the golden age is sure to come, and that is why he is patient and content to be a slave."

"Content to be a slave!" repeated Bran. "Does this God teach him to be a coward, then?"

"Nay, my Anicetus is not a coward," said Hilda, quickly, for she had learned in her native land that bravery was the highest virtue, and cowardice the greatest vice.

"But he must be a coward if he is patient and content to be a slave," objected Bran.

VICE: *weakness*

But Hilda still shook her head.

"Felicita said Anicetus would be a brave man to face the anger of Plautius, our master, by letting me come to you, and he is brave, too, although he is a slave," said the little girl, warmly.

Bran looked puzzled. He could not understand this old man at all; and this last account of his being willing to brave trouble himself to show kindness to them was still more perplexing. "I wonder how it is he is so kind; *we* cannot pay him, for we are poor and friendless," he said, half aloud.

"Perhaps God's messenger told him to be kind to us;" Hilda said; "for God knows all about us, you know, and how we came from Britain, for He helped us along the road, Anicetus says. Do you think he told that soldier to take the chain off your ankle when He saw it bleeding? I think He did, for there were some soldiers listening to Paul; and

Anicetus says the great captain Pudens loves this God."

"A soldier listen to this message of the golden age—this message of love!" said Bran, in astonishment.

"Perhaps the soldiers will be as glad as the slaves to hear of it," suggested Hilda.

But Bran shook his head. "These Roman soldiers are as fierce as Britons, and like fighting and killing men and women. It pleases their gods."

"But it would not please this great God," said Hilda, decidedly.

There was a pause for a few minutes, and then Bran asked how long Anicetus had known this messenger Paul, and whether he was rich and noble like their master Plautius. It was evident that more than his curiosity had been aroused by what he had heard, and he wanted his little sister to leave him, that she might go with Anicetus again and hear more about this wonderful message.

But Hilda was not willing to do this. "I can't go away and leave you, Bran," she said. "Let me tell you every bit I know to-day, and perhaps Anicetus will tell me some more tomorrow, for Felicita said I must go and help her pound the honey and oatmeal in the morning; and I shall see him then, because he has charge of the prison, you know, and must let me out."

"What else can you tell me?" asked Bran, rather discontentedly.

"I learned some words that Anicetus says Paul has written on parchment—'Jesus Christ came into the world to save sinners.' That is the gospel message, he says, and he made me say it over and over, that I might never forget it. Will you learn it too?" asked the little girl.

"I don't know; I want to hear something about it first. Tell me what you know, Hilda," he said.

But the child was at a loss how to begin

her story. "Anicetus could tell you better than I can," she said.

"But I don't want to hear it from Anicetus," said Bran, angrily. "I want you to tell me. Who is Jesus Christ?" he asked.

Hilda had had a long conversation with her old friend upon this the previous evening, and so she could answer his question. She went on to tell him how the Lord Christ came down from heaven and became a poor man, and at last died on the cross like a slave, that He might save men, slaves and nobles, from their sin—not only the punishment of it, but the love of it.

It was not so easy to do this, for the words "sin" and "love" were strange ones to both of them, and Hilda had to explain their meaning to Bran, as Anicetus had done for her; and she was rewarded for the pains she had taken to remember everything by seeing how deeply interested her brother became as she went on with the story.

There was little else talked of all day, and
Bran forgot to grumble over his own trouble
and hardships in listening to the account of
the sufferings endured by the Lord Jesus
Christ.

"And it was all for us, Bran," said Hilda,
in a sorrowful whisper, as she concluded her
recital.

Tears were standing in Bran's eyes now,
fierce and angry as he often was, for he
could understand better what those sufferings had been than his little sister could, for
she knew nothing of the awful sight he had
witnessed only the day before. He had gone
with two or three companions in search of
some amusement beyond the city gates, and
a little way out beyond the walls they had
come to a piece of waste ground, where several crosses were standing. Bran did not no-
tice them at first, but on drawing nearer he
saw the body of a man hanging on one, and
then his friends told him it was the way the

Romans put their slaves to death, so that he knew it was indeed a slave's death the Lord Jesus had suffered, as well as a cruel and agonizing one. "God's Son died the death of a slave to save us!" he slowly repeated, and then there followed a long silence, during which it was evident he was pondering this fact.

At length he said, "Hilda, I cannot understand it; I must ask Anicetus to tell me more when the Saturnalia is over."

"Perhaps he will take you to hear God's messenger teach. Would not you like to see this great teacher, Paul?"

"Yes, I should like to see him; but it is the message I want to hear now, and why God's Son had to die the death of a slave to save us. Why was it, Hilda?" he asked.

"Because He loves us, Anicetus says."

Bran slowly shook his head, and a softened look came over his whole countenance. "He couldn't love me," he slowly uttered.

AGONIZING: *extremely painful*

"Yes, He does, Bran, I am sure," said his sister, quickly; "Anicetus said He loves me, and—"

"Yes, Hilda, He might love you—anybody might—because you are kind and gentle; but I am fierce and cruel. He did not die to save me; there can be no golden age for me."

"Yes there is, Bran; I am sure there is," said Hilda, tearfully.

But Bran still shook his head. "No, no," he said; "there is no quarrelling, no fighting in the golden age, and I always liked fighting."

"But suppose God took the love of fighting out of you; made you hate it like you hate being a slave?" suggested Hilda.

"But he couldn't, Hilda; I'm a Briton, and all Britons love these things," and the old hard despairing look came over his face again.

But his little sister would not give up. Again and again she repeated what Anicetus had told her—that Christ died for all;

and at last she gained from him the promise that he would ask Anicetus himself to tell him more of these things.

With this promise, Hilda lay down on the heap of straw in the corner, and went to sleep for the night, wondering whether God knew she was staying in prison with Bran, and could not enjoy her holiday as she had expected to do.

The next morning she was sent for to help Felicita and the other slaves in preparing her mistress's bath, for so many different soaps, oils, and perfumes were used by the Roman ladies in bathing, that it was quite a difficult business, and occupied several slaves to attend to this alone.

Hilda could not do much beyond running errands and helping to compound the different mixtures; but being quick to learn, and willing to do anything, she was told she was too handy now to be spared, more especially as everybody wanted to get this needful piece of work done to enjoy their holiday. Felicita, who superintended the work of the rest, was in a great hurry this morning, for she had promised to meet some friends early, and so when Hilda was sent to fetch some goat's milk from a distant part of the house, she was told to make haste and not to stay talking to anyone.

Hilda obeyed this command; but in her hurry she spilled the milk just as she reached the chamber where they were busy preparing and compounding the materials for the bath. A sharp slap for her carelessness was given by Felicita, and she was sent for some more.

This accident seemed to put everybody out of temper, and Hilda was scolded by one and slapped by another and pushed aside by a third, until she too grew angry, and in a moment of passion she willfully threw down a crystal vase that was used for perfume, and broke it in a hundred pieces.

A look of consternation overspread every face as they saw the scattered pieces of this costly toilet ornament, and Felicita gasped, "What shall I do? my mistress will be so angry when she hears of this being broken."

"She won't ask for it today," said one; "but she will have Hilda whipped when she does."

Poor Hilda had already repented her passionate outburst, and now stood frightened and ashamed, looking at her work of destruction. At the mention of being whipped, however, she burst into tears.

"Oh, don't tell her I did it; say it fell down," she sobbed; and turning to Felicita, she said, "Don't let me be whipped, and I won't break it again."

"You *can't* break that again, naughty girl; but if I say the serpent came in here and broke that, will you promise never to get into a passion again?" said Felicita.

She had never heard that it was wrong to speak falsely. The stories she had been

CONSTERNATION: *sudden alarm and dismay*
TOILET: *dressing table*

told of the lives of her gods made her rather believe that they would be pleased with a falsehood, if it were only told cunningly and successfully. She knew too that her young mistress would be far less angry if she thought the mischief had been done by one of her pet serpents than by her slave, for these reptiles were often far more tenderly cared for in the houses of these proud Romans than the men and women who served them.

So Felicita promised to lay the blame of what had happened upon the serpents, whose cage was close by, and Hilda promised never to be careless or passionate again. Everybody said she deserved to be punished, however, and no one objected to her returning to her brother today, for she ought to lose her holiday after doing such mischief.

"She doesn't deserve to hear my stories about Father Saturn and the golden age," said Felicita, reproachfully, as she gathered up the pieces of crystal from the marble floor.

"I have heard of a better God than Saturn," said Hilda; "one who is sure to give us a golden age by-and-by."

All the slaves had left off their mixing and pounding to stare at her while she said this.

"Has the foolish little Briton gone crazy?" said one.

"Her brother drank too much wine yesterday, I heard; perhaps she has been doing the same," suggested another.

Felicita, however, seized her by the arm, and shook her. "What do you mean, you wicked little Briton, by insulting our great Father Saturn," she said, angrily. "Don't you know he is the only god who cares for slaves; that we have to thank him for our great holiday?" she demanded.

"The great God who made heaven and earth cares for slaves," said Hilda, boldly.

"Who?" The question came from several.

Felicita had dropped her arm, and stood looking at her in blank astonishment, as she, too, asked this.

"The Lord God Almighty—that is His name—and He loves us and takes care of us; He is the God of love," said Hilda slowly, but firmly.

"The God of slaves and the God of love!" said Felicita, slowly; but she did not grow angry with Hilda again, but said, pityingly, "Poor child, poor little Briton, you are a stranger here, or you would know there is no god for slaves now since the reign of Saturn has ended."

"But this great God—"

"Don't talk about that any more," interrupted Felicita; "I am older than you, and have lived all my life in this great city, and I tell you there is no god for slaves."

CHAPTER IV

HILDA'S CONFESSION

THE Saturnalia came to an end all too soon for some; but Bran and Hilda were thankful when the seven days' holiday was over, for they were both heartily tired of the gloomy prison where several days had been spent. Bran was also anxious to speak to Anicetus about the strange things Hilda had told him, and he soon found he was not alone in this desire.

As he was standing near a group of other slaves preparing some vegetables he overheard one of them say, "Have you heard what all the women are talking about—the golden age that is coming?"

"I heard that the little Briton, Hilda, had been telling them some strange things about the God of slaves."

"But there is no god for slaves!" said two or three together; "who would care for the poor when they can hardly take care of themselves?"

"Well, old Anicetus seems to have told the child all this," said another. "And I should like to know the truth of it."

"Anicetus! What does he know of these things?"

"More than the rest of us, it seems; and it has changed him, too, for he has been kind and considerate to everybody lately, and he was hard and unfeeling before."

A similar conversation was being carried on among the women slaves about the same time, for it had been discovered that Hilda had learned her strange knowledge from Anicetus.

Hilda herself was in some trouble this morning, for news of her passionate out-

burst and the destruction of the costly vase
had reached the ears of her old friend, and
he had told her that she ought to confess
what she had done to the lady Agrippina,
her mistress. Anything more dreadful than
this Hilda could not imagine, for the lady
was stern and haughty in her manners towards everybody, and rarely spoke to her
slaves except to find fault or scold them, so
that the poor little girl dreaded making this
confession, even more than the beating that
must follow.

But Anicetus said that, hard as it might
be, she must do it; it was the first piece of
work God had given her to do for Him, and
she must do it.

"But this cannot be work for God!" said
Hilda, in astonishment. "The vase was not
His, or else—"

"Nay, but you were wrong to grow passionate and break this crystal; and it would be
worse if Felicita told a lie to hide it, for this
would be a great sin," said Anicetus.

"Does He care so much about little things like that?" said Hilda, pouting.

"Sin is not a little thing," said the old man; "if it had been it would not have cost what it did, the heavy price that was paid to ransom us; for it was because of this, because men had been false as well as cruel, that the Lord Jesus Christ died upon the cross," and the old man shuddered at the thought of that awful agony which he himself had once barely escaped.

But Hilda still shrank from the dreadful ordeal of confessing her fault to her mistress, until Anicetus said, "The Lord Jesus died on the cross to save you, and you tell me you believe this, and want to love and please Him, and yet you will not tell the truth about this vase for His sake." The old man spoke in a sad and grieved tone that touched Hilda very deeply.

"It is so hard to do this," she said, with a little stifled sob.

"And was it easy for Christ to bear the pain of the cross, do you think? And yet He bore it willingly for your sake, to save you from your sins; and you say it is too hard to leave off sinning for His sake," said Anicetus, gravely.

"Yes, I will. I will tell Agrippina, my mistress, that I threw down the vase; I will tell her while Felicita is combing her hair, and I am rubbing her feet this morning," said Hilda, impetuously.

"And the Lord will stand by you, little one, and be your help," said Anicetus, in an encouraging tone. "This is your first battle with sin, Hilda, and it is a hard one, I know; but the Lord, who died to redeem you from its power, will give you the victory."

Anicetus had just spoken these words when Felicita called her to assist in preparing the bath, and while this was being done the conversation turned upon the strange news that had gone abroad in the house—that

IMPETUOUSLY: *suddenly*

Anicetus said there was a God who loved slaves.

It had long been known that the old man did not worship any of the Roman deities, but went to hear what he called "the gospel" from one Paul; but that this message of love had any particular meaning for slaves had not been talked of. That there was no god for slaves, had always been accepted as a positive fact; and so to hear that this great God cared as much for the oppressed, down-trodden, despised crowd who were bought and sold like cattle in the market, as He did for their handsome emperor Nero in his purple robes and jeweled crown, was some-thing so astonishing, so altogether unheard of, that Felicita might well be pardoned for saying the old man had grown childish and foolish, and that some should laugh at the idea of a golden age coming in which slaves should have a share.

Hilda was asked what she had heard about this, and whether she believed the wonderful

DEITIES: *gods*

story; but beyond giving the mere answer to these questions the little girl did not care to talk this morning, for her mind was occupied with the thought of the trial that awaited her. No inquiry had as yet been made for the broken vase, and Felicita had begun to hope that her mistress had forgotten it entirely, as she had not missed it from her toilet-table, and Hilda had urged this as a reason against confessing her faults when talking the matter over with Anicetus. But the old man would not take this as an excuse; she must be honest and upright in all things, he said, and so Hilda had promised not to wait longer, but to confess what had happened, this very morning. The other slaves wondered what could make her so silent, and one or two asked if she had broken another vase; but no one knew of her resolution to tell the whole truth concerning what she had done, until, as she sat on the floor chafing Agrippina's feet, she suddenly said, "Oh, my mistress, I have been a very naughty girl."

CHAFING: *rubbing*

For a moment everybody in the room suspended their occupation in surprise, while the lady looked down at Hilda's frightened, tearful face, and said, "You have been a naughty girl? What have you done?"

"I broke the crystal vase," said Hilda.

The lady glanced at the ornaments arranged on the table before her and frowned.

"How did you break it?" she asked, rather sternly.

"I threw it down," said Hilda, her voice almost choked with sobs, while Felicita forgot her task of combing the lady's hair, and the slaves arranging the dress she was about to put on paused in their work to stare at the little girl in blank amazement.

Agrippina herself was so astonished at receiving this voluntary confession from one of her slaves, the honesty displayed was so unheard of; that she forgot to be angry in her amazement.

SUSPENDED: *paused*

"What made you tell me this, child?" she asked at length, after looking at her in silence for some moments.

"The Lord Jesus Christ loves me, and I want to love Him," said Hilda, venturing to raise her eyes towards her mistress's face.

The lady looked towards her principal waiting-maid for an explanation. "What does she mean, Felicita?" she demanded.

"Nay, I do not know. She broke the vase truly; but I know not what she means now."

"Such honesty is beyond the understanding of a slave," said Agrippina, sharply.

Felicita did not reply, but went on with her employment of brushing out her mistress's hair, and then shaking gold dust over it to increase its bright luster, while Agrippina sat silently pondering what she should do under the extraordinary circumstances. Hilda ought to be whipped, certainly, and it would be a breach of discipline to omit this punishment; but the

BREACH: *violation*

lady was curious to know more about the whole matter, and especially who the Lord Jesus Christ was, for she had heard that the child was an utter stranger in Rome. So her first question to Hilda was where she had heard of the Lord Jesus Christ. "Is He in your native land or in Rome?" asked the lady.

"He is in heaven," answered Hilda, "in the golden city."

"But where did you hear of this?" said Agrippina, looking puzzled.

"Anicetus took me to hear the message of the great God from the mouth of His messenger Paul, who is a prisoner here in Rome."

"And it was what this prisoner said that made you confess breaking my vase?" said the lady, still more puzzled.

"Anicetus said I must tell you all about it for the sake of what the Lord Jesus suffered to save me from my sins," said Hilda, in a subdued voice.

"What did He suffer?" asked the proud lady. The questioning of her little slave seemed to amuse and interest her.

"He died on the cross for our sins, because we had broken God's commandments, and could not go to heaven, to the golden city, unless our sins were washed away."

"He died on the cross! Then He was only a slave Himself," said the lady, contemptuously.

"No, He is God's Son," said Hilda, gaining confidence as she went on. "Anicetus says that He left His throne in heaven and came down to die for men's sin, because there was no other way of saving them, and—"

"Then Anicetus knows more about this than you do?" said the lady.

"Yes, he has often heard Paul speaking about these things, and he has learned to love the Lord Jesus Christ."

"Then I will send for him to tell me something concerning this strange matter. Go,

Hilda, and fetch the old man; I have a short time to spare before going to visit my friend Julia, and will hear more about this."

Hilda hardly knew whether to be pleased or vexed at thus being sent to summon her old friend; but from the meaning glances exchanged among the other slaves she feared that she had said or done something likely to bring down the lady's anger upon all of them. She therefore walked very slowly and deliberately to look for Anicetus, and her worst fears were confirmed when she saw the look of alarm that overspread the old man's face as he received the message.

"The lady Agrippina would have me tell her this gospel-message!" he said slowly. "Nay, nay, but I am no worthy messenger. I cannot show forth the riches of the Lord's grace as can our great teacher Paul."

"But you can tell her 'Jesus Christ came into the world to save sinners,'" suggested Hilda; "and perhaps she will go and see Paul for herself."

But Anicetus shook his head. "I am not worthy to deliver this great message; I cannot become the teacher of men," he said, in great embarrassment.

"But you will hasten to the *atrium* and tell my mistress something of this," said Hilda; and she hastened back, leaving the old man to follow her more slowly.

Poor Anicetus had longed for and dreaded such an opportunity as this; longed to tell others of the glorious message he had heard, and accepted, but in his deep humility he shrank from doing it lest he should deliver it unworthily, and thus prejudice men's minds against its acceptance rather than recommend it. This had deterred him from telling even his fellow-slaves until little Hilda came, and in her he found a responsive listener.

Now, however, that he was summoned to tell his young mistress this same message, all his doubts and fears about his own worthiness and fitness for the task returned

DETERRED: *restrained*

upon him, and it was with a slow and lingering step that he followed Hilda to the *atrium* where Agrippina awaited him.

The young lady stood near the images of the household deities, the Lares and Penates, when the old man entered.

"What is this new worship, this new religion, you have been teaching Hilda, my British slave?" asked the young lady, imperiously; and she ordered her slaves to fetch a pile of cushions, upon which she reclined, and prepared to listen to the old man's recital.

What could he do but tell her as well as he was able the story of God's love to man, as he had heard it from the lips of Paul? With a silent, heartfelt prayer for help for the right words to be given him, he began the wondrous story; and soon Agrippina had forgotten the flight of time, or that her maids still stood behind her couch awaiting her commands, and listening with the

LARES AND PENATES: *Roman household gods*
IMPERIOUSLY: *commandingly*

same breathless interest as their mistress to the old man's simple yet eloquent words, as he told of man's creation and fall, and of the redemption that had been provided in Christ for the salvation of all.

"Truly this is a strange, a marvelous story, worthy the attention of the wise and noble, as well as of slaves," she said as he concluded.

"The message is sent to all, noble lady," answered Anicetus; "and many of the great and wise are now learning its truths from the lips of Paul."

"And you say he is a Jew imprisoned here in Rome by his own countrymen for teaching these things?"

"Yes, he is a prisoner, but dwelling in his own hired house, where any may visit him without fear and without question," answered Anicetus.

The lady pondered for a minute, but at length she said, "You shall conduct me to this strange prisoner when there is again an assembly in his house, and meanwhile I will make some further inquiry about this matter." She then dismissed Anicetus, and commanded another slave to order her litter at once.

"Hilda shall alone attend me this morning," she said, turning to Felicita; and so when the litter was announced the little girl was lifted to a seat beside her mistress, and borne by the attendant slaves to another fashionable quarter of the imperial city.

To the little slave, so unused to this mode of traveling, being carried through the streets on a luxurious couch, screened from view by half-transparent silken curtains, that yet enabled those inside to see all that was going on, was simply delightful; and she was half sorry when the short journey came to an end, and her mistress alighted to pay a visit to her friend Julia.

"You are to come with me, Hilda," said the lady, "for I may want you to help me remember what Anicetus said;" and they were then ushered into the presence of Agrippina's most intimate friend.

"I have heard something this morning, Julia, that is worth the telling; something really new to break the monotony of our dull, miserable life," said the young lady, as soon as she was seated.

"Is life so miserable then?" asked Julia.

"Yes, indeed it is; I get tired of living, and often wish I could die, if we only knew what came after death," said her visitor, with a deep drawn sigh.

"Ah! but no one does know that. It is a leap in the dark, and no one can tell us what lies beyond in the land of shades."

"Yes, they can," answered Agrippina, eagerly; "there has been a light discovered piercing this darkness at last, and our old slave Anicetus has been telling me this morning of a wonderful messenger now in Rome, who has been sent by the greatest

LAND OF SHADES: *land of the dead*

of all gods to declare His will, and to teach men how to love and serve Him."

"That would be news indeed for Rome if it were true," said Julia; "but, my Agrippina, it is impossible. Our wise men for ages have been trying to break through this darkness, to be able to give us some certain knowledge about the world of shades, whether we do live again, or whether we perish like the brutes."

"Well, this man is charged with a message that makes this quite clear; and I have come to ask you this morning to go with me the next time there is an assembly at his house, to hear more of this matter."

Julia hesitated for a moment. "Have you asked your mother, Agrippina?" she asked.

"What is the use, Julia? You know she is so absorbed with her grief for poor little Claudia, that she can think of nothing else," said her visitor, crossly.

"You will take your slaves with you, then?"

said Julia, noticing that her friend had only brought Hilda.

"Yes, Anicetus shall go with me as well as Felicita and Hilda. I will take a hundred if you like, Julia, if you will only promise to come with me."

"Yes, I will come," said Julia; "but now tell me all you have heard about this."

Assisted by occasional reminders from Hilda, to whom she appealed, Agrippina told the story she had heard from the lips of Anicetus, not omitting to mention how it was she had been induced to make this inquiry by the strange honesty of Hilda in confessing that she had broken the vase. An hour was spent in this way, and then the friends parted with the promise to go and hear Paul the following day.

Chapter V

A Roman Household

AGRIPPINA thought she was conferring a great honor and distinction upon this unknown teacher, Paul, when she, with her friend Julia, went to his prison-house, attended by Anicetus and several of her waiting-maids. To her surprise, however, there were other litters standing near the door quite as elegant as her own, and when she entered the *atrium* she found that she was not the only patrician lady who desired to hear more of this new doctrine. She had thought, too, that some deference would be shown to her at once, that there would be some recognition of the great social difference existing between her and the slaves who

DEFERENCE: *respect or courtesy*

came to listen to this good news, and she felt half offended when she saw that those present as high in rank as herself were sitting beside slaves and freedmen indiscriminately.

The hall was nearly full when she entered, but a roughly-made seat was soon placed for the accommodation of herself and friend, as well as her attendant slaves. Felicita, however, was afraid to sit down in the presence of her mistress, and the idea of occupying the seat near her was too preposterous to be entertained for a moment. Anicetus, too, felt uncomfortable, and knew not what to do, and Hilda drew near his side, and looked up wistfully in his face to be guided by him, for the old man had told her that there in God's house all men were free and equal; but the presence of their haughty mistress seemed strangely to have altered this today.

At length Anicetus stooped and whispered, "Hilda, we will stand today; we are here to attend Agrippina, and it is our duty to pay all due honor to her as our mistress;"

INDISCRIMINATELY: *without noticing a difference*
PREPOSTEROUS: *absurd*

and so the old man did not press forward
to take his rightful seat as a member of the
church, but stood with Felicita and the rest
behind the two ladies.

All externals were, however, soon forgotten, for the bent, worn figure of the man
upon whom all eyes were fixed was seen
slowly advancing with the soldier to whom
he was attached, and soon words of prayer
were ascending to God, earnest supplica-
tions on behalf of those who knew Him to
be their Father and their God, that they
might love Him and trust Him more fully, and comprehend more of the riches of
His grace, and for those who knew Him
not, who had never heard His name, but
were seeking Him blindly, and almost
hopelessly, that they, too, might learn
to love and trust Him as their God; that
Christ Jesus might be revealed to them as
the great deliverer from sin and iniquity,
and they, too, might wash their robes, and

EXHORTATION: *message*
ELOQUENCE: *skillfulness and persuasiveness*

make them white in the blood of the Lamb.

Then came an exhortation, the eloquence of which alone astonished Agrippina and her friend; but this was not the only reason why they listened with such breathless, rapt attention, for there were other eloquent men in Rome besides Paul, but he brought tidings that, "Kings and prophets waited for, And sought, but never found;"[1] for the gospel alone can bring "life and immortality to light;"[2] and this wonderful truth held the two ladies enchained, so that they were quite unconscious of the lapse of time, and even of their strange surroundings.

When the sermon was ended, and some made a movement to retire, Agrippina said, "I wish my mother could hear these words, for they would comfort her more than anything else, I am sure."

"Yes, if they are only true, this world must be but a vain show and of little account," said Julia.

---

[1] Words from *How Beauteous Are Their Feet*, a hymn by Isaac Watts (1674-1748)

[2] II TIMOTHY 1:10

"Nay, but we must serve Him here, Paul said; before we go to that other world where all the ranks and distinctions of this will pass away," replied Agrippina, as she turned to leave the hall with the rest.

There was quite a crowd of litters near the door, and most of them were borne towards the fashionable part of the city again, but Agrippina decided to go in another direction.

"I want to look on Claudia's funeral urn; my mother has not been able to go the last few days, and I would fain see that the flowers have been renewed," she said, in explanation to her friend.

Julia could not accompany her. "My presence is needed at home," she said; "but I shall come to hear this stranger again shortly."

"And I will persuade my mother to come with me tomorrow," said Agrippina, as they parted, each wondering what effect this strange teaching would have upon the other.

WOULD FAIN: *desire to*
RENEWED: *replaced with fresh ones*

Agrippina was thinking of what she had heard until after the city gate was passed, and the grove of myrtle and olive-trees reached; and here stood the funeral cypresses, beneath the dark shadow of which had been placed the funeral urns containing the ashes of her ancestors for many generations. Claudia, her little sister, had been the last laid upon the funeral pyre; and though fresh-woven flower-wreaths had been laid upon her tomb, there was not a word of hope in the inscription engraved upon it: "Claudia was cruelly snatched away from my arms by the curse of death; and now there is no hope in life for her sorrowing mother."

Agrippina read this again, as she had read it many times before; but instead of repeating as usual, "Death is a cruel curse," she whispered thoughtfully to herself, "I wonder whether there is hope for my mother in this new religion?"

FUNERAL CYPRESSES: *tall, thin evergreen trees; often planted at grave sites by the ancient Romans*
PYRE: *a fire built to burn the body of a dead person*

The stainless white marble was carefully dusted by Anicetus, and fresh flowers placed around the urn; but Agrippina seemed strangely forgetful of the surroundings, as well as of her attendant slaves today, for the tears fell from her eyes, and she said half aloud, "I wish my little sister had heard the wonderful words I have heard today." She forgot to find fault or scold any of her attendants, so absorbed was she in her own reflections; and when she reached home, instead of ordering her bath to be prepared, she went in search of her mother, to tell her the strange, glad tidings that there was a fuller, happier, and more joyful life beyond the grave. Quite as earnest was the discussion in the slave quarters of the house as in the *peristyle* that evening, when, most of the work being done, Bran and Hilda, with several of the others, sat together listening to the account given of the day's visit to Paul, the prisoner.

"He told of freedom and gladness, of redemption from sin through the death of God's Son; and I will learn what this redemption means," said one of Agrippina's litter-bearers, who had followed his mistress into the prison-house to hear what he could concerning the good tidings that had brought the proud lady into this strange neighbourhood.

"Anicetus can tell you what it is, what this redemption means," said Bran, trying to seem unconcerned. There was little hope that he would be able to go out and hear this great teacher himself, for he was drudge to the cook, and a hard life he had, a life that was making him more hard and fierce and bitter each day. He wanted to hear what the old man said about the wonderful truths he had heard of from Hilda; but he would not ask for himself, although he had made up his mind to do so while he was in prison, and so he gladly

DRUDGE: *an assistant who does menial work*

suggested that someone else should apply to Anicetus.

"Yes, it was Anicetus and the little Hilda there, that first brought this tale amongst us," said another, who himself secretly longed to hear more concerning the matter.

"Then we will ask the old man to be our teacher, and we will come here each evening to listen to what he can tell us of this new God—the God who loves slaves."

This was the point of attraction for these poor, oppressed, downtrodden men and women; and to them the gospel was glad tidings indeed, and willingly did they listen to what Anicetus told them when he was at last prevailed upon to speak.

In his humility the old man had shrunk from doing this before; but now that he had done it once he was ready enough to tell the story of the life and death of Christ, and did not fail to impress upon his hearers that they must themselves not only hear what the

Lord had done for them, but strive to follow His example in obedience to His commands.

"What are His commands?" asked one of the anxious listeners.

Anicetus thought for a minute, and then answered, "Believe in Him,[1] and 'love one another.'"[2]

"And is this all?" asked two or three together.

"Yes; this love is the fulfillment of the Divine command, for if we believe in Him we shall try to love and serve Him; and if we love each other there will be no evil-speaking, no false-witness, no robbing or defrauding any man, but we shall frankly own our faults if we have done amiss, even as we confess our sins to God."

Bran looked at his sister as the old man said this, for he had heard that Anicetus had laid this command upon her, at which he felt inclined to blame the old man, and

---

[1] John 3:15-18 [2] John 13:34

DEFRAUDING: *cheating*

OWN: *admit*

think the conditions of this new religion were very hard, too hard for slaves to comply with. To confess a fault to their master or mistress would often involve them in cruel punishment that otherwise might be escaped. It was evident that some such thought as this was passing through the minds of the other auditors now, for they looked at each other, and then at Anicetus, as they, too, recalled that Hilda had been told that she must confess how the vase had been broken; and several heads were shaken as they recollected how often they indulged in little thefts and little deceits, without which they persuaded themselves they could not live.

Anicetus seemed to divine what was passing through their minds, for he said, "My friends, the Lord Jesus must set us free from the chains of our sins, as well as from the earthly bondage that must end in a few years. Each of us have fettered ourselves with

AUDITORS: *listeners*
RECOLLECTED: *remembered*
DIVINE: *understand*

a chain of sin that the power of Christ alone can break. In one, this may be a fierce, passionate temper; in another it may be dishonesty, the small thefts, the daily little robbery of a few sesterces or a little fruit; to another it may be the deceit of appearing to be what we are not."

He was himself a slave, and knew their temptations and trials, and knew that the things he had mentioned were "the sins that so easily beset them;"[1] for how could it be otherwise but that falseness and hollowness should be the result of such cruel harshness as they were exposed to, unless the grace of God should make and keep them upright and truthful? More than one among that little company felt discouraged and ready to give up all future thought about this new religion, for to give up their sins was impossible.

"I thought you said it was a religion for slaves, and this God loved us," grumbled one.

[1] HEBREWS 12:1
FETTERED: *bound*
SESTERCES: *brass coins*

"And He does love you, loves you so well that He gave His Son to die for you; but He died to save you *from* your sins, not that you might live *in* them," said Anicetus, calmly.

"Nay, but this religion is not fair and equal," objected one who prided himself on being more clever than many of his companions; "it presses hard on the slave to the advantage of our masters, and yet you say this God loves the slaves."

"I said not that our God loved the slave *more* than the master; but that they were equal in His sight. There is the same command for the rich as for the poor; only 'love one another' may mean something quite different to our masters, yet quite as hard to fulfill as it is for us to be truthful and honest and gentle," said Anicetus, firmly.

"Well, I should like to see a master or mistress do their part first," said the slave; and he asked one to join him in a game of hazard, and Anicetus turned sadly away as one after another went to join in the sport.

Bran, however, did not join in it this evening. He drew Hilda into a corner, and, unobserved by the rest, he asked his little sister some further questions upon the same subject. At length he said slowly, "Would the Lord Jesus help me to break my passionate temper?"

"Yes, Bran, I am sure He would; I asked Him to do it, and I am sure He will," replied the little girl, quickly.

But Bran was by no means so sure.

"I am bad," he said; "I have more sins to be forgiven than you, Hilda."

"Yes, but not more than Jesus can forgive," she replied. "I wish you could hear what Paul says about this; perhaps you will be able to go some day," she added.

"Perhaps I shall," repeated Bran; but it was not said very hopefully.

"You will try to do what Anicetus says, you will begin to pray to the Lord Jesus to help you, won't you?" said Hilda, pleadingly.

Bran looked down into the earnest, up-turned face of his little sister.

"You are trying to serve Christ, and to enjoy this heaven Anicetus speaks of?" he said, questioningly.

"I think heaven is beginning already; I feel so glad today," answered Hilda.

"Then I will try to share it, too. I will begin to pray, as old Anicetus says I must."

Bran spoke very resolutely, and Hilda knew that he meant it, but neither thought that his resolution would so soon be put to the test. The little girl had risen from her low seat, and was about to leave her brother, when one of those who had been playing suddenly turned and asked whether they were going to try this new faith.

"It will just suit a fierce Briton, this religion of love," he said, mockingly.

Bran's face grew scarlet at the taunt, and he hastily rose to confront his tormentor; but the next minute he sat down again, though Hilda noticed that his hands were clenched, and the veins in his forehead were swollen with repressed passion.

"Poor Bran, it is hard!" she whispered, gently; "but the Lord Jesus is helping you, I know."

Finding that Bran was not disposed to quarrel and fight as usual, his tormentor walked away in search of some other amusement, and Hilda persuaded her brother to come with her in search of Anicetus, that he might answer some questions that she could not. With the old man Bran would be safe for the present; and rejoicing over her brother's first victory, the little girl returned to her duties, feeling happier than she had ever been before.

REPRESSED: *restrained*

CHAPTER VI

DUTIES FOR ALL

WHILE Anicetus was telling the glad tidings of salvation to his companions, Agrippina was relating to her mother what she had heard concerning the hope of another life beyond the grave.

"Could there be another life, a life of happiness, for my little Claudia?" said the elder lady, eagerly; but the next minute she fell back upon her couch and covered her face with her hands.

"My mother, it is true, I am sure," said Agrippina, in a voice strangely kind and gentle for her; "this Paul, the messenger of the gospel, is no ordinary man, but learned and eloquent as Seneca himself; and it is for the sake of these truths that he is now imprisoned."

"A stranger and a prisoner bring such tidings to Rome!" exclaimed the lady. "Nay, nay, but surely this God would choose a noble messenger to tell such joyful news."

"And is he not noble, my mother, when for this he is willing to suffer imprisonment at the hands of his countrymen rather than keep the joyful news to himself, as they would have him?"

"Is it for this he is detained a prisoner? Nay, nay, Agrippina, but our great and wise men would surely welcome him; and our emperor Nero would set him at liberty, that he might teach our senators this new truth," said her mother, doubtingly.

"But our emperor has doubtless heard that this new God loves the poor and the slaves quite as much as the rich and noble,"

SENECA: *a Roman philosopher in the first century* A.D.

said the young lady, who was determined to interest her mother favorably if possible.

"He cares for slaves!" repeated the elder, in a tone of astonishment. "Nay, nay, such good news is not for them."

"It did not please me to hear of this, my mother; but it is true, and in this man's prison-house he will have no difference, saying it is God's house; while God's Word is taught, and all men being equal in His sight, slaves and patricians shall sit together; and I found that high-born noble ladies were sitting beside slaves and freedmen of the poorest sort."

The elder lady lifted her hands in horror. "What will become of our city if the slaves hear of this—hear that they are of as much account as their masters?"

"They have heard it already; but, Mother, this strange religion, while it teaches that all men are alike in God's sight, teaches the slaves to be honest and obedient. It was my little British waiting-maid, who told me how she broke my essence vase, that first roused my curiosity in this matter; for, as you know, the slaves usually hide such things as long as possible, and then make excuses and tell endless falsehoods to conceal their faults."

"And this little Briton did not!" exclaimed her mother.

"Nay, she did not wait for me to discover its loss, but told me she had thrown it down in her temper; and when I asked why she told me this, she said she wanted to love this God whom Paul preaches."

"It is strange, most strange," said the lady; "I too should like to hear more concerning this doctrine."

"I can tell you a little, my mother; but I would that you should hear this prisoner Paul for yourself," said Agrippina. "Anicetus, whom we know to be our most faithful slave, is a believer in this new God, and he says

ESSENCE: *perfume*

that it is all true about the happy land beyond the grave; and that the whole com-
mandment of this God is to love Him and
love one another."[1]

"Nay, but surely we are not asked to love
our slaves?" objected the lady.

"Yes; we are to be kind, just, and considerate towards them," answered Agrippina.

Her mother looked scornful. "And *you*
can believe *this!*" she said; "believe in a God
who takes the part of slaves against their
masters, and tells *them* of an eternal life in
heaven?"

"But the promise is not for them alone,
my mother," said Agrippina, quickly; "and
which of our gods can tell us of a life beyond
the funeral urn?"

"I would that they could give us some
hope of this," said the lady, with a deep-
drawn sigh.

"They cannot; but, my mother, you will
go to hear this messenger of One who has

[1] MATTHEW 22:37-40

'brought life and immortality to light?'" said her daughter, anxiously.

"I don't know, I cannot promise; I will think of what you have said." And with this Agrippina was obliged to be content.

She was very anxious to go again and hear the strange preacher, in spite of his surroundings and the presence of so many slaves; but she wanted her mother to go with her, not only because she wished her to hear the joy-giving words of the teacher, but because she could go more frequently herself without comment from her friends if it were thus sanctioned by her mother.

To the elder lady the news of such a teacher being in Rome, the fact that her painful doubts and fears, and questionings concerning the future life, could be set at rest, was so very startling that she could think of little else during the remainder of the day; and before the following morning dawned she had made up her mind to

SANCTIONED: *approved*

accompany Agrippina to see this God-sent messenger.

Meanwhile, Agrippina had been thinking over little Hilda's confession about the broken vase and the words she had herself uttered concerning loving one another and the duties it involved. If this law of God obliged Hilda to be truthful and candid, surely it had some obligation for her. If they were to be truthful, she ought not by her harshness to make them afraid of telling the truth; she ought to be kind and considerate, instead of haughty and tyrannical.

It was perhaps the first time the young lady had ever indulged such thoughts, for she had always been taught that slaves existed solely for the gratification and use of the rich, and therefore she had treated them as being quite different from herself in everything. This gospel that Paul preached, however, recognized them as having the same thoughts and feelings, the same hopes and

TYRANNICAL: *acting like a tyrant*
GRATIFICATION: *pleasure*

fears, as the richest; and Agrippina began dimly to see that if she was to be a sharer in the lofty hopes and joys this faith made known she must recognize her slaves as those to whom kindness and consideration must be shown, even if she could not love them yet.

The two ladies, with a retinue of slaves, went to the prison-house of Paul the next day, and the elder lady was as shocked as her daughter had been at the arrangements made for the accommodation of the hearers; but this and all other discomforts were forgotten when she heard the apostle exhort his disciples "not to sorrow as those without hope"[1] because one of their number had died.

"She is not dead, but the dusky curtain that hides the fuller life from us hides her now from our view, for she has passed to the other side, and is now in the presence of the Lord Christ, who loved her and gave

[1] I THESSALONIANS 4:13

RETINUE: *group of attendants*

Himself for her, that she might inherit this eternal life."

This was the message Paul had for his hearers today; and one of them who had sorrowed without a ray of hope for more than a year listened to it as though it was a message from her lost child.

"My poor little Claudia, is it possible she can be living even now?" said the lady, excitedly, as she turned towards her daughter.

Agrippina held up her finger warningly, for again that eloquent voice was heard speaking. It was the word of prayer this time, and Paul spoke to God as if in His very presence, as a son to a loving father, as a friend might speak to a friend on behalf of those dear to the hearts of both.

Anicetus watched his mistress as she entered her litter, and he saw the tears flow from her eyes more than once; and the old man's heart was raised in prayer for her as well as for another whom he knew to be struggling to follow in the steps of Christ and prove himself a servant of his Lord.

Mistress and slave, the high-born and civilized Roman and the half-savage Briton, were alike in many particulars, for both Bran and Agrippina had to conquer a proud, ungoverned temper, and to neither would the victory be an easy one. Little Hilda, too, had discovered that one victory does not mean a conquest, for now that she stood so high in her mistress's favor, Felicita more frequently found fault and took less pains to show her how to perform her various duties. Her younger companions, likewise, grew jealous of her popularity, and made all sorts of excuses for keeping her pounding and mixing when she had been used to run off and spend half an hour with Bran, and this tried her temper more sorely than anything.

In this way several months passed, and it was noticeable that not one of Agrippina's waiting-maids had been whipped, and that she was far more easy to please than she had been before. Felicita remarked the fact, but chose to attribute it to anything rather than the true cause, for she hated these Christians, as the disciples of Paul began to be called, for it was through this that Hilda had gained so much favor. There were others, too, in the household who hated the name, but not all. The cook had been so struck with the change in Bran that he spoke of it to Anicetus. "He was the most sullen, ill-tempered fellow when he first came, that I told the noble Plautius one day that I hoped he would soon sell him and get me another to do his work."

"He was not taught to do kitchen work," remarked Anicetus; "those straight, strong limbs are fit for something else than plucking nightingales or pounding sage."

"That is true enough," assented the cook; "but what work could he be entrusted to

ASSENTED: *agreed*

do? If he were a litter-bearer and something offended him in the street, he would drop the litter and turn to fight the offender; and if he had been made one of the guard doubtless he would have struck Plautius himself in less than a week."

"But the lad is improving now, and I hope you will mention it to Plautius if you have the opportunity," said Anicetus.

A few days afterwards the old man was sent for to attend his master in the library. "I am going to make some changes in the household," said Plautius. "I am obliged to sell ten of my slaves to pay a debt that has long been owing, and I want you to help me select those who can best be spared."

It was not a pleasant task, and the old man almost trembled with anxiety as he recalled what had been said a day or two before concerning Bran, but still he hoped to be able to shield him from this trial. But, alas! for his hopes, the first one his master mentioned was "that obstinate Briton who had given so much trouble."

"He was rather troublesome," assented Anicetus, "but he has improved so much lately that he will soon be one of the most trustworthy and valuable—"

"So much the better," interrupted Plautius; "he will fetch a higher price if he is tamed. Now for the next, Anicetus."

But the old man was determined to make another effort on poor Bran's behalf. "The Briton would not fetch so much in the market as some others we could spare," he said.

But his master had decided this matter, and would hear nothing the old man could say. Nine others were finally selected from the rest, and Anicetus was directed to send them to the dealer the next day.

The news of what was about to take place soon became known in the household, and Bran was one of the first to hear of it. At first he only smiled and thought it was another trick to put him out of temper, but when Hilda came to him crying and repeating the same tale he feared it was too true. For a minute he turned pale, and his nostrils worked convulsively as he dropped the bird he was plucking and seized Hilda's hand muttering, "I can't bear this."

"Let us go to Anicetus," said Hilda, through her fast-falling tears; "he will tell us what we ought to do, Bran," and she drew her brother towards the little chamber where the old man usually sat.

"Anicetus, is it true that I am to be sold?" asked Bran, after he had stood silently looking at the bowed figure of the old man for some minutes. Slowly the head was raised at last, and Bran repeated his question.

"I hope not, my son; I hope to save you this parting with your sister," said his friend, in a voice faint with emotion.

Bran knew not why Anicetus should be so disturbed as he seemed; and it was evident their presence was not desired just now, but no word was spoken beyond this, that they were not to be troubled, he would save them if it was possible.

Later in the day Anicetus again sought his master. This time it was to ask what price he expected to receive for each of the slaves.

"I don't know how the market may be, Anicetus; make as good a bargain as you can for me," said Plautius, with careless good-humor.

The old man looked down at the marble pavement and then at his master again. "I have served you faithfully for many years," he said; "what price would you be willing to give if you were buying me now?"

"Anicetus, what do you mean? I have no thought of selling you, my good fellow; I could not spare *you!*"

"Bran would serve you as faithfully as I have, and if you will let me take his place in the market I shall be thank—"

"Anicetus, you are crazy! Whoever heard of such a thing? What would you do among strangers now, an old man like you?" interrupted Plautius.

"I should be sorry to leave you it is true; but I love and serve a Master in heaven who gave Himself for me, and He has said that we are to love one another, even as He loved us."

Plautius stood gazing at the old man until his daughter came into the *peristyle*, and then turning to her he said quietly, "I am afraid Anicetus is losing his wits, Agrippina."

The young lady turned then and looked at the old man. "What is it, Anicetus?" she said; "are you ill?"

He smiled faintly at the question. "Nay, I did but speak of my Master in heaven to the noble Plautius. I would fain follow in His footsteps and take the place of Bran in the market tomorrow, for if he is sold it will break his sister's heart, but there is none to sorrow after me."

"Bran to be sold!" exclaimed Agrippina, turning towards her father as if for an explanation.

Plautius looked annoyed. "I am going to make some changes in the household, Agrippina," he said, shortly; and then turning to Anicetus, he said, "I cannot listen to such a foolish thing as you propose; let this Briton be sold with the rest."

Chapter VII

Light at Eventide

ANICETUS went back to his usual quarters with mingled feelings of relief and regret; relief that he had not to seek a new home where harder work than he could perform would probably be expected from him, and yet with keenest regret that he had not been allowed to give his almost worn out and solitary life in exchange for the young Briton's.

How Bran was to be told of the failure of the effort made in his behalf he did not know. He had no intention of telling him the offer he had made to Plautius, he would simply say that their master was obliged

EVENTIDE: *evening*

to raise money, and he must be sold with the others. It was easy to decide what to say; but how was he to say it? How was he to bear the speechless agony that he knew Bran would suffer at the thought of parting with his sister?

But Anicetus had learned where to seek and find strength for every emergency. Paul had taught his converts to "be careful for nothing, but in everything by prayer and supplication with thanksgiving let your requests be made known unto God."[1]

Not only for himself did he pray, but for Bran and Hilda too, and so deeply absorbed was he in this that he did not hear or see the curtain hanging near the entrance slowly drawn aside, admitting little Hilda, and so she stood there listening with bated breath while the old man pleaded for her brother and herself. What she heard was enough to convince her that his effort to save Bran had failed, and that in a few hours she must part

[1] PHILIPPIANS 4:6

BATED BREATH: *breath held*

with her brother; perhaps forever, for who could tell where he might be carried when he again left the slave-market?

This thought so overcame poor Hilda that, quite forgetting the errand upon which she had been sent, she threw herself upon the floor with a burst of sorrow which completely roused Anicetus from the absorption of his prayer, and he hastened to raise her from the ground and try to comfort her. But what could he say to stay the poor child's tears as she sobbed, "I can't bear it, I can't part with Bran; my mother is dead, and everybody except Bran, and I must go with him!"

"Hush, hush! little one, the Lord Jesus Christ is alive—alive forevermore—and He will go with poor Bran," said Anicetus, trying to soothe the poor child's grief.

"Anicetus, if He is alive, can't *He* save Bran—can't He prevent him from being sold tomorrow?" asked Hilda, suddenly pausing between her convulsive sobs.

ABSORPTION: *concentration*
STAY: *stop*

The old man seemed somewhat puzzled, but at length he said, "Yes, little one, the Lord Jesus could save him from going away tomorrow, but—"

"Then why did we not ask Him, Anicetus?" interrupted Hilda.

"I have asked this; but my prayer is not to be answered in the way I asked it," said the old man with a sigh.

"Never mind, we will ask again. Ask God to save him which way He thinks best," said Hilda, as she released herself from the old man's arms, and put herself in the posture of prayer.

When this was concluded Hilda had dried her eyes, and for the first time recollected that she had been sent to summon Anicetus to the presence of Agrippina her mistress. She started as she remembered this. "I must not stay longer," she said; "my mistress sent me to bid you attend her, but I had well-nigh forgotten it;" and without waiting for the old

POSTURE: *position*

man's reply, she left the little chamber and hurried through the marble corridor to the more stately portion of the house.

Meanwhile, Agrippina was impatiently waiting her return and the coming of Anicetus; and as the minutes flew by she began to pace up and down the tesselated pavement in a way that made the attendant slave standing near the entrance tremble with apprehension, for he could see the flush of angry impatience deepen in the lady's cheek; and he thought poor Hilda's chance of escaping a whipping this time was very small indeed.

But the slave saw only the outward sign of anger and imperiousness. He knew nothing of the battle that was even now going on in the lady's mind as she paced up and down the hall—a battle that had to be fought again and again—for her proud passionate temper could not be conquered easily, or subdued without a long, hard

TESSELATED: *checkered*

struggle. Had Hilda thus transgressed a few months before, another slave would have been sent after her, not to bring her back, but to take her to be whipped without giving her an opportunity to account for her delay, or even appeal against this severe punishment; and why this had not already been done, the waiting, watching slave was at a loss to know.

At length the heavy curtain over the doorway was hastily pushed aside, as Hilda, breathless and confused, almost rushed into her mistress's presence, instead of entering with the lowly reverence becoming her station.

For a moment Agrippina looked stern and severe as she said, "What has happened, Hilda? Why have you been so long?"

"I—I—oh, Bran is to be sold tomorrow!" said Hilda, and then she burst into tears just as the curtain was again moved aside to admit Anicetus.

BECOMING HER STATION: *suitable for her position*

The lady turned to him for an explanation, for Hilda was sobbing now as though her heart would break, although it was against the rule for a slave to show any personal emotion in the presence of her mistress. "What has happened to trouble the child?" asked Agrippina.

"I will ask pardon for her, my mistress, for she is indeed in sore trouble concerning her brother, who is to be sold tomorrow morning."

"And whose place you sought to take for the sake of this poor child!" said Agrippina, quickly.

"My days are short, and it matters little now whether pain or ease be my portion, since I shall see my Savior face to face very soon," said Anicetus; "but for Bran, it may be, there is a long life before him, and I fain would see him well-grounded and settled in the love of Christ ere he goes forth where he may never hear His name again."

"It was for this I wished to see you. My father tells me ten of the slaves must be sold tomorrow, and Bran is one of these, I suppose?"

"Yes, most noble Agrippina, he is to be sold with the rest, and yet it will be a great loss to sell him just now, for he is little more than half-tamed; but by-and-by one so strong and active and faithful as Bran will be, would be worth far more."

"Will he be worthy of freedom, think you, Anicetus?" asked the lady, softly.

Hilda heard the question, and almost held her breath in doubtful surprise as to what its real meaning could be. Anicetus, too, was amazed, and for a minute or two could only look at Agrippina in blank astonishment as he answered, "Bran is free-born, and would value freedom almost more than life."

"Then he may regain it some day," said the lady. "Mind, I do not say he will, for it will depend upon himself; but I have learned from the gospel, which I at first thought was wholly on the side of slaves, that masters have duties as well as servants, and so I would fain do what I can to prove my love to the Lord Jesus Christ by helping my slaves. Will you take this, Anicetus, and sell it for me? The price you get for it will purchase Bran, and he will be my own slave in the future."

As she spoke Agrippina handed the old man a costly gold bracelet set with diamonds, and at the same time gave him a waxen tablet on which she had written a few words with her gold stylus, giving him the authority to dispose of this, in case the jeweler to whom she directed him to take it should think it had been stolen.

Hilda had been almost forgottten, but as Anicetus bowed, and was about to leave the *atrium*, she ran forward and seized him by the arm. "You have forgotten to thank God," she said. "Don't you know we asked Him to

PROVE: *demonstrate*
STYLUS: *a pointed tool used to write letters in wax*

save Bran, and He is going to do it, and so we ought to thank Him as soon as we know it?"

Anicetus looked at her flushed, earnest face, and then glanced towards the stately lady, as though he would apologize for her. But Agrippina did not want apologies now, whatever she might have done a short time before.

"Hilda is right, I think, Anicetus," she said; "for it is not to me, but to Him who has taught me this gospel of love, that the thanks are due. Come, thank Him for us all," she added—"for saving Bran from the slave-market, and for saving me from the slavery of selfishness."

Thus requested, Anicetus could not refuse, and so with outspread arms and uplifted hands, in a few fervent, grateful words, he returned thanks for the great mercy God had bestowed upon them in sending His Son to redeem them from the curse of sin and self, and that He had taught them by His Spirit to love one another, through which Bran would be saved much sorrow and many temptations, and by which the hearts and faith of many would be strengthened to trust in His love more fully through this answer to their prayers.

Anicetus then went out to dispose of the bracelet, while Hilda attended her mistress to her mother's chamber, for she was very ill, and would not be left entirely to the care of slaves. At least, Agrippina would not leave her to them now, although she would doubtless have shrunk from entering a sick chamber before, and considered she had done her whole duty if she inquired after her welfare once a day, and sent an extra offering to the temple of Fortuna on her behalf.

All this, however, had been strangely changed by the reception of the gospel, and Agrippina often sat by her mother's bedside, reading from a parchment roll some of the

FORTUNA: *the Roman goddess of good fortune or luck*

writings of Paul—letters that had been sent
to distant churches, which had been copied
and distributed among his converts here in
Rome; or she would hold the draughts of
cooling snow-water to her mother's parched
lips, while she whispered some words of
cheerful hope uttered by their great teacher
in his last sermon.

The look of weary unhappiness had passed
from the invalid's face, and in spite of her
sickness she looked calm and peaceful, as
she whispered, "I shall soon know what this
eternal life is, my Agrippina, for I shall see
my Savior face to face."

"Nay, but, my mother, you will be spared
to serve Him here in Rome, I trust," said
Agrippina, quickly.

But the invalid shook her head. "It is better as it is," she said. "'Life and immortality have been brought to light by the gospel.' It is what I have been groping after
all my life, but never found until now; and

SNOW-WATER: *melted snow*

perhaps I should fail to do all this gospel requires of me, for I am not strong, Agrippina—not so strong as you, but a good deal older. It would be harder for me to give up the worship of the gods than for you, and I might fail at last, and so it is better as it is."

Agrippina started. "Give up honoring our old gods," she said; "are we bidden to do that, my mother?"

It may seem strange to us in these days, such a question as this; but Agrippina had been so occupied in fighting the enemy within, that she had given no thought to this outward form of evil, the worship of idol gods. But to the eyes of her who was already near the borders of the grave this great difficulty had been clearly revealed.

"Agrippina, the God Almighty is the only true God, and therefore all false gods must be given up if we would serve Him," said the invalid.

Agrippina looked up quickly. "Is this the meaning of so much that I have failed to understand in the teaching of Paul?" she asked.

"Doubtless it is, my Agrippina; but you will not give up the Lord Christ for Juno and Jupiter now, for Christ has redeemed me and brought 'life and immortality to light,' but they can give me no hope of a future life."

Of that future life beyond the grave Agrippina and her mother often spoke. Death had no terrors for the invalid now, and she begged Agrippina not to yield to excessive grief when she should be taken from her sight. Often, too, they united in prayer on behalf of Plautius, who, as yet, knew very little of the change in his wife and daughter, except that they went to hear a strange teacher, who had lately come to Rome, and he only regarded it as a new whim of Agrippina's, of which she would grow tired by-and-by.

JUNO: *a Roman goddess and the wife of Jupiter in Roman mythology*

He was, however, greatly concerned about his wife's illness, and several physicians were called in to see her. He was likewise anxious that she should not know anything about the sale of the slaves, a fact that he had communicated to Agrippina, so that she was somewhat surprised when her mother asked several questions about Hilda.

She had dismissed the child, and sent her to Felicita, so that her troubled face should not be seen, and yet the invalid's first question was about her. "She had a brother, too, had she not, a half-savage Briton, whom no one could tame?" said the lady.

"Yes; but Bran will be tamed now, for Anicetus tells me he has learned much of the gospel from his little sister, and is trying earnestly to conquer his angry, passionate temper, and learn all that is required of him."

"Poor fellow, he finds slavery very hard, I doubt not," said the invalid. And then, after a pause, she said, "Agrippina, I owe a great debt to this little British slave girl."

"To Hilda!" repeated Agrippina. "Yes, my mother, I have thought if it had not been for Hilda's faithfulness in confessing she broke the vase, we might never have heard this great teacher, or the glorious gospel he comes to proclaim. Truly we do owe a great debt to this child."

"Agrippina, it is a debt I should like to repay as far as I can; I should like to set this girl or her brother free."

"My mother, it shall be done; I will purchase Bran's liberty, and you shall pay the price for Hilda," said Agrippina.

"I should like it done before I go. I should like the parchments made ready soon," said the elder lady. "I will talk to Plautius about this matter tomorrow, and it may be I can tell him also of the 'life and immortality brought to light.'"

Chapter VIII

Conclusion

B Y the sale of Agrippina's bracelet Anicetus had more than sufficient to redeem Bran; but it was necessary that he
should once more stand in the slave-market,
although this was a mere form, for Anicetus
had privately told the merchant he would
repurchase him at a fair market value. This
was explained to Bran, and it was a great
relief to him; but still the very fact that he
was in the power of another, and could be
bought and sold like the dumb cattle, was
in itself so keenly felt that it was not surprising that he walked with drooping, downcast
head toward the marketplace where the

DUMB: *unable to speak*

money would be handed over and he passed back to the charge of Anicetus. The old man himself could not fully sympathize with this feeling of the young Briton, for he was born a slave, and therefore knew nothing of the joys and aspirations of freedom, and he thought Bran ought to be more grateful than he appeared to be for Agrippina's kind consideration. When the exchange had been effected and he returned home, he found that he was not to return to his work in the kitchen, for he was now the private property of Agrippina, and it would be his duty to attend her litter as bearer or footman whenever she went out. This was certainly more to his taste than his late employment; but he now had so much idle time upon his hands that he often knew not what to do with himself, for as the days went on Agrippina went out less and sat in her mother's chamber more, until at last she barely went anywhere but to the meetings held in the prison-house of Paul. These meetings Bran could attend himself now, and he was soon to be admitted a member of the church as well as his sister and mistress.

Hilda had grown to be the sunbeam of the slave quarter in this Roman household, as she had been of the rude mud hovel at home, for had she not all she wanted now? Bran was with her; and if he sometimes looked sad and anxious, he still assured her he was happy, happier than he had ever been in his life before. Agrippina was kind and considerate towards her slaves and it had awoken such a great desire in many of their hearts to know more of the religion that could so change their haughty mistress that they forgot their jealousy of the little British slave in their desire to learn the truth which she had first made known to them all.

So pleasant and easy was the little girl's life where all were trying to fulfill the gospel of love in their treatment of each other that Hilda often assured Bran that the golden age had come, or was about to begin, but he gravely shook his head, although he did not like to sadden her happy spirit.

"No, no, Hilda," he said; "we must wait a while longer, for are we not slaves? and although our mistress is kind we may be sent to the slave-market tomorrow."

"Then it would be quite the golden age if we were free, would it not?" asked Hilda.

Anicetus heard the question. "No, little one; the happy time will not come until the Lord Jesus has conquered all sin, and—"

"But, Anicetus, you tell us we must each try to conquer sin in our own hearts," interrupted Hilda; "and don't you think God gives us a little golden age there all to ourselves?"

The old man looked puzzled for a moment, but at length he said, "Yes, dear child, I think He does sometimes give us a foretaste of the peace and happiness that shall be full and abundant by-and-by in His kingdom."

"It is like a little golden age in the house as well as in our hearts," said Hilda; "for now that Felicita is trying to love the Lord Jesus she doesn't scold me, and nobody is afraid to prepare the bath for our mistress, as we used to be, and Bran is almost happy, although he is a slave still."

What that golden age in its fullness and glory would be one of that household would soon know, for slowly and peacefully Agrippina's mother was passing away, and Plautius had at last been forced to believe that the parting was near. At first he had refused to listen to his wife's account of life and immortality being brought to light by Jesus Christ; but when he saw with what fearless peace she could look forward to what had been such a dreadful horror of darkness before, he could not but acknowledge that there must be a power in this gospel beyond that possessed by any of their gods, and he had several times gone secretly to the wonderful prisoner Paul to hear for himself the glad tidings of salvation.

That this was not without effect was proved, too, by his consenting at last that Bran and Hilda should both be presented with their freedom, for he had resolutely opposed this at first, saying it would make the other slaves dissatisfied. Now, however, he not only consented, but sent for a lawyer to draw up the parchments necessary for this without delay, for he was anxious to gratify his wife's wish in this matter.

Not a day too soon was this business completed, for while the lawyer was in the *atrium*, having brought the parchments for their signatures, Plautius was summoned by a message that his wife was taken worse. At the sight, however, of the parchments which he carried in his hand she rallied a little and whispered to Agrippina to send for Bran and Hilda.

The two young Britons, who did not know why they were sent for, came in trembling with fear at first, for Bran had whispered that he was going to be sold again when he heard that a lawyer with parchments had been admitted to their master's presence.

Agrippina, however, motioned them to come forward; and while she helped to steady the feeble fingers of the invalid as she wrote with the reed the last words needful to set the two at liberty, she bade them both kneel down at the side of the couch, for she thought her mother would like to say a few words to them. But the feeble strength was too far exhausted when the reed fell from her fingers, and it was only after a lengthened pause that she was able to whisper just above her breath, yet loud enough for all to hear as she gave Bran his parchment, "Christ has made you free!"

She looked with a loving smile at Hilda as she placed the second parchment in her hand and said, "Still be faithful, and meet me in the better world."

Agrippina then hurried them to the door, and as she raised the curtain she said, "You are both free; you are no longer slaves," and then she returned to her mother's side; for she could see the end was drawing near.

When Bran had sufficiently recovered from his astonishment to be able to speak, he could only look blankly at the parchment he still held in his hand, and utter, "Free, free! no longer a slave! What does it mean, Hilda?"

But the little girl was still thinking of the solemn scene she had just witnessed, and the tears were in her eyes as she slowly shook her head and whispered, "Let us go to Anicetus; he will tell us all about it."

The old man was not surprised to see the two enter his chamber with the parchments

FREE AT LAST!

in their hands, for he knew what was intended.

"What does it mean?" he repeated, slowly, looking first at Bran and then at the parchment; "it means that you are free, boy; free, now, body and soul," he added, softly.

"And this makes me free?" said Bran, touching the parchment as he spoke.

"This is the proof of it; but this parchment alone could not free you."

"No, it was my noble mistress, Agrippina, that made me free," said Bran; then suddenly looking up, he asked, "Why, then, is this parchment necessary, Anicetus?"

"That others may know it, likewise. Listen, boy, this is what our great teacher Paul was trying to make us understand but yesterday: our master Christ frees us from sin and the power of Satan, but the works of faith and love are necessary to prove to others that we are His servants instead of the bond-slaves of Satan. Loving one another, and works of kindness and faithfulness, cannot save us; but they are the proofs that Christ has saved us, even as this proves you are now free."

"Go away from you and my dear mistress?" uttered Hilda. "Nay, nay; then I do not want this parchment," she said, throwing it on the ground and bursting into tears.

Bran, too, looked disconcerted, and the document suddenly lost half its value in his eyes, as he thought of parting with the friends who had been so kind to him of late. At length he said, "Anicetus, I do not wish to leave my noble mistress; nay, I feel more anxious to serve her now, if I may do so still. Will you ask her this?" he added.

But Anicetus had no opportunity of preferring this request, for even while they were talking death had entered the mansion, and she who had lived all her life in fear of it had welcomed it at last as the messenger sent to take her to her Father's home above.

DISCONCERTED: *unsettled*
PREFERRING: *presenting*

For a few days all were busy in preparation for the funeral, for the wealthy Romans did not bury their dead, but burned them, and spices had to be prepared, and mourning women hired to do honor to the departed, for Plautius would not have a rite omitted, and Agrippina, with Felicita and her other maids, kept a constant watch beside her mother's body until it was carried away. Not, however, in useless hopeless grief was this time of mourning spent now, but in meditating and talking of the new and glorious hope so lately revealed, that there was another, a purer, nobler, happier life beyond the grave, where friends would meet in the presence of Christ, never to be separated again.

As soon after the funeral as he could, Anicetus asked an audience of his mistress, and told her of Bran's distress at the thought of leaving her service. The lady was deeply moved at this proof of the Briton's faithful devotion, and also somewhat surprised.

RITE OMITTED: *ceremony left out*

"I thought he was most anxious to be free," she said.

"He was," answered Anicetus; "I never saw anyone so glad, so deeply grateful as this boy is, and it is out of this gratitude that he desires to pay you more faithful service as a free man than he can as a slave."

"But I wish him to be free, and to fit himself for freedom, which he cannot do wasting his time in idle games with the rest. As for Hilda, she had better remain as she is for the present," said the lady.

"Then you would bid Bran seek employment in the city?" said Anicetus.

"Yes; I would have him learn to weave or dig, or do anything he may think good," replied Agrippina.

The thought of being free to use the strength God had given him was a joyful one to Bran, and he readily agreed to hire himself to a gardener or vine-dresser; but he made one stipulation with Anicetus, which was that he should be allowed to come some-times and help to carry Agrippina's litter, and thus render her some service in grati-tude for his deliverance.

Although Bran had seen very little of Ro-man agriculture, he was not long in learn-ing how to dig and plant in Roman fashion, and he had soon formed a plan of return-ing to his own country when Hilda should be old enough to undertake the long jour-ney across the mountains. Now that he had learned to love the Lord Christ, he longed to carry this gospel, this love-message, to his own countrymen for as it had subdued and tamed his savage, evil temper, so it could change and conquer theirs, and this plan he was not long in imparting to his faithful friend, Anicetus, as well as his sister.

She, of course, entered warmly into the project although she did not like the idea of leaving her mistress, even to return to Brit-ain, and comforted herself with the thought

IMPARTING: *telling*

that it was not likely to happen for several years.

In this, however, she was mistaken, for Agrippina became acquainted with the British princess Claudia, while attending the meetings of the prisoner Paul; and on hearing that she was about to return to her native country, she told her how greatly she was indebted to little Hilda, and that she was anxious to return home with her brother.

The next day Bran was summoned to the palace where Claudia lived, and, after several questions, was asked if he would like to return to Britain in the service of Claudia, who wanted him not only to plant her own gardens, but to teach his young countrymen something of Roman agriculture. Her offer was eagerly accepted by Bran; and Hilda, when she saw his joy, would not damp it by her regret at leaving the dear friends by whom she was surrounded. Bran, however, knew it would not be easy for his sister to part with these, and he whispered, "It will not be for long, Hilda, only a few years, and then we shall all meet in our Heavenly Father's house; and if we can go to Britain and tell our friends there that there is a Savior for them too, a God who loves them and desires their love, we ought to go, for we should be miserable slaves still if Paul had not come to Rome to tell all men this message of grace, and bid them seek this God of love, who sent His Son to die for them."

"Yes, we will go," answered Hilda; "and Anicetus will pray for our Britain as he prayed for you, Bran; and it may be that there will come a day when Britons as well as Romans will love our Lord Jesus Christ, and then, Bran, that will be the golden age for Britain."

THE END

ABOUT THE AUTHOR

Emma Leslie (1837-1909), whose actual name was Emma Dixon, lived in Lewisham, Kent, in the south of England. She was a prolific Victorian children's author who wrote over 100 books. Emma Leslie's first book, *The Two Orphans,* was published in 1863 and her books remained in print for years after her death. She is buried at the St. Mary's Parish Church, in Pwllcrochan, Pembroke, South Wales.

Emma Leslie brought a strong Christian emphasis into her writing and many of her books were published by the Religious Tract Society. Her extensive historical fiction works covered many important periods in church history. Her writing also included a short booklet on the life of Queen Victoria published in the 50th year of the Queen's reign.

Emma Leslie Junior Church History Series

The Magic Runes
A Tale of the Times of Charlemagne

One day, in 782 A.D., young Adalinda is startled to come upon a Saxon family in the forest where she lives with her father. The family is in desperate need but the husband, Godrith, is suspicious of Adalinda's offers of help, especially when he learns that she is a Christian. He well remembers how Charlemagne's "Christian" soldiers burned his village and killed or captured so many of his people because they refused to convert to Christianity. Will Adalinda and her father be able to show Godrith a different picture of Christianity?

For Merrie England
A Tale of the Weavers of Norfolk

In the fall of 1357, a Flemish weaver travels around the countryside in England, at the request of the king, seeking apprentices to learn his trade. Along the way he meets a prosperous wool merchant with two sons—big, strong, sixteen-year-old Roger and small, crippled, thirteen-year-old Tom. The merchant is eager to advance his elder son but the weaver feels drawn to the intelligence of young Tom who is seen only as a burden and a curse. When Roger suddenly disappears one evening, the weaver sees his opportunity to help Tom, but will Tom's father agree to his startling plan?

www.SalemRidgePress.com

SOLDIER FRITZ
A Story of the Reformation

Young Fritz wants to follow in the footsteps of Martin Luther and be a soldier for the Lord, so he chooses a Bible from the peddler's pack as his birthday gift. When his father, the Count, goes off to war, however, Fritz and his mother and little sister are forced to flee into the forest to escape being thrown in prison for their new faith. Disguising themselves as commoners, they must trust the Lord as they wait and hope for the Count to rescue them. But how will he ever be able to find them?

Through Stress and Strain
A Story of the Huguenot Persecution

These are difficult times for the Huguenots in France when Jules Marot comes to visit his brother's family and brings bad news about their young son, Jacques. Huguenot schools and churches are being torn down and these faithful Christians are forbidden to gather for services. The Marot family watches in dismay as many families who were once fervent in the faith give in to the pressure to convert to the "king's religion." As the persecution intensifies, can the whole Marot family, including their sons, Jacques and François, learn to trust God more than ever before?

www.SalemRidgePress.com

EMMA LESLIE CHURCH HISTORY SERIES

GLAUCIA THE GREEK SLAVE
A Tale of Athens in the First Century

After the death of her father, Glaucia is sold to a wealthy Roman family to pay his debts. She tries hard to adjust to her new life but longs to find a God who can love even a slave. Meanwhile, her brother, Laon, struggles to find her and to earn enough money to buy her freedom. But what is the mystery that surrounds their mother's disappearance years earlier and will they ever be able to read the message in the parchments she left for them?

THE CAPTIVES
Or, Escape from the Druid Council

The Druid priests are as cold and cruel as the forest spirits they claim to represent, and Guntra, the chief of her tribe of Britons, must make a desperate deal with them to protect those she loves. Unaware of Guntra's struggles, Jugurtha, her son, longs to drive the hated Roman conquerors from the land. When he encounters the Christian centurion, Marcinius, Jugurtha mocks the idea of a God of love and kindness, but there comes a day when he is in need of love and kindness for himself and his beloved little sister. Will he allow Marcinius to help him? And will the gospel of Jesus Christ ever penetrate the brutal religion of the proud Britons?

www.SalemRidgePress.com

EMMA LESLIE CHURCH HISTORY SERIES

OUT OF THE MOUTH OF THE LION
Or, The Church in the Catacombs

When Flaminius, a high Roman official, takes his wife, Flavia, to the Colosseum to see Christians thrown to the lions, he has no idea the effect it will have. Flavia cannot forget the faith of the martyrs, and finally, to protect her from complete disgrace or even danger, Flaminius requests a transfer to a more remote government post. As he and his family travel to the seven cities of Asia Minor mentioned in Revelation, he sees the various responses of the churches to persecution. His attitude toward the despised Christians begins to change, but does he dare forsake the gods of Rome and embrace the Lord Jesus Christ?

SOWING BESIDE ALL WATERS
A Tale of the World in the Church

There is newfound freedom from persecution for Christians under the emperor, Constantine, but newfound troubles as well. Errors and pagan ways are creeping into the Church, while many of the most devoted Christians are withdrawing from the world into the desert as hermits and nuns. Quadratus, one of the emperor's special guards, is concerned over these developments, even in his own family. Then a riot sweeps through the city and Quadratus' home is ransacked. When he regains consciousness, he finds that his sister, Placidia, is gone. Where is she? And can the Church handle the new freedom, and remain faithful?

www.SalemRidgePress.com

EMMA LESLIE CHURCH HISTORY SERIES

FROM BONDAGE TO FREEDOM
A Tale of the Times of Mohammed

At a Syrian market two Christian women are sold as slaves. One of the slaves ends up in Rome where Bishop Gregory is teaching his new doctrine of "purgatory" and the need for Christians to finish paying for their own sins. The other slave travels with her new master, Mohammed, back to Arabia, where Mohammed eventually declares himself to be the prophet of God. In Rome and Arabia, the two women and countless others fall into the bondage of man-made religions—will they learn at last to find true freedom in the Lord Jesus Christ alone?

THE MARTYR'S VICTORY
A Story of Danish England

Knowing full well they may die in the attempt, a small band of monks sets out to convert the savage Danes who have laid waste to the surrounding countryside year after year. The monks' faith is sorely tested as they face opposition from the angry Priest of Odin as well as doubts, sickness and starvation, but their leader, Osric, is unwavering in his attempts to share the "White Christ" with those who reject Him. Then the monks discover a young Christian woman who has escaped being sacrificed to the Danish gods—can she help reach those who had enslaved her and tried to kill her?

GYTHA'S MESSAGE
A Tale of Saxon England

Having discovered God's love for her, Gytha, a young slave, longs to escape the violence and cruelty of the world and devote herself to learning more about this God of love. Instead she lives in a Saxon household that despises the name of Christ. Her simple faith and devoted service bring hope and purpose to those around her, especially during the dark days when England is defeated by William the Conqueror. Through all of her trials, can Gytha learn to trust that God often has greater work for us to do *in* the world than *out* of it?

www.SalemRidgePress.com

Emma Leslie Church History Series

LEOFWINE THE MONK
Or, The Curse of the Ericsons
A Story of a Saxon Family

Leofwine, unlike his wild, younger brother, finds no pleasure in terrorizing the countrside, and longs to enter a monastery. Shortly after he does, however, he hears strange rumors of a monk who preaches "heresy". Unable to stop thinking about these new ideas, Leofwine at last determines to leave the monastery and England. Leofwine's search for inner peace takes him to France and Rome and finally to Jerusalem, but in his travels, he uncovers a plot against his beloved country. Will he be able to help save England? And will he ever find true rest for his troubled soul?

ELFREDA THE SAXON
Or, The Orphan of Jerusalem
A Sequel to Leofwine

When Jerusalem is captured by the Muslims, Elfreda, a young orphan, is sent back to England to her mother's sister. Her aunt is not at all pleased to see her, and her uncle fears she may have brought the family curse back to England. Elfreda's cousin, Guy, who is joining King Richard's Crusade, promises Elfreda that he will win such honor as a crusader that the curse will be removed. Over the years that follow, however, severe trials befall the family and Guy and Elfreda despair of the curse ever being lifted. Is it possible that there is One with power stronger than any curse?

DEARER THAN LIFE
A Story of the Times of Wycliffe

When a neighboring monastery lays claim to one of his fields, Sir Hugh Middleton refuses to yield his property, and further offends the monastery by sending his younger son, Stephen, to study under Dr. John Wycliffe. At the same time, Sir Hugh sends his elder son, Harry, to serve as an attendant to the powerful Duke of Lancaster. As Wycliffe seeks to share the Word of God with the common people, Stephen and Harry and their sisters help spread the truth, but what will it cost them in the dangerous day in which they live?

www.SalemRidgePress.com

Emma Leslie Church History Series

BEFORE THE DAWN
A Tale of Wycliffe and Huss

To please her crippled grandson, Conrad, Dame Ursula allows a kindly blacksmith and his friend, Ned Trueman, to visit the boy. Soon, however, she becomes suspicious that the men belong to the despised group who are followers of Dr. John Wycliffe, and she passionately warns Conrad of the dangers of evil "heresy". He decides to become a famous teacher in the Church so he can combat heresy, but he wonders why all the remedies of the Church fail to cure him. And why do his mother and grandmother refuse to speak of the father he has never known?

FAITHFUL, BUT NOT FAMOUS
A Tale of the French Reformation

Young Claude Leclerc travels to Paris to begin his training for the priesthood, but he is not sure *what* he believes about God. One day he learns the words to an old hymn and is drawn to the lines about "David's Royal Fountain" that will "purge every sin away." Claude yearns to find this fountain, and at last dares to ask the famous Dr. Lefèvre where he can find it. His question leads Dr. Lefèvre to set aside his study of the saints and study the Scriptures in earnest. As Dr. Lefèvre grasps the wonderful truth of salvation by grace, he wants to share it with Claude, but Claude has mysteriously disappeared. Where is he? And is France truly ready to receive the good news of the gospel of Jesus Christ?

www.SalemRidgePress.com

Fiction for Younger Readers

MARY JANE – HER BOOK
by Clara Ingram Judson
Illustrated by Francis White

This story, the first book in the Mary Jane series, recounts the happy, wholesome adventures of five-year-old Mary Jane and her family as she helps her mother around the house, goes on a picnic with the big girls, plants a garden with her father, learns to sew and more!

MARY JANE – HER VISIT
by Clara Ingram Judson
Illustrated by Francis White

In this story, the second book in the Mary Jane series, five-year-old Mary Jane has more happy, wholesome adventures, this time at her great-grandparents' farm in the country where she hunts for eggs, picks berries, finds baby rabbits, goes to the circus and more!

www.SalemRidgePress.com

Historical Fiction for Younger Readers

AMERICAN TWINS OF THE REVOLUTION
by Lucy Fitch Perkins

General Washington has no money to pay his discouraged troops and twins Sally and Roger are asked by their father, General Priestly, to help hide a shipment of gold which will be used to pay the American soldiers. Unfortunately, British spies have also learned about the gold and will stop at nothing to prevent it from reaching General Washington. Based on a true story, this is a thrilling episode from our nation's history!

MARIE'S HOME
Or, A Glimpse of the Past
by Caroline Austin
Illustrated by Gordon Browne R. I.

Eleven-year-old Marie Hamilton and her family travel to France at the invitation of Louis XVI, just before the start of the French Revolution. There they encounter the tremendous disparity between the proud French Nobility and the oppressed and starving French people. When an enraged mob storms the palace of Versailles, Marie and her family are rescued from grave danger by a strange twist of events, but Marie's story of courage, self-sacrifice and true nobility is not yet over! Honor, duty, compassion and forgiveness are all portrayed in this uplifting story.

www.SalemRidgePress.com

Historical Fiction by William W. Canfield

THE WHITE SENECA
Illustrated by G. A. Harker

Captured by the Senecas, fifteen-year-old Henry Cochrane grows to love the Indian ways and becomes Dundiswa—the White Seneca. When Henry is captured by an enemy tribe, however, he must make a desperate attempt to escape from them and rescue fellow captive, Constance Leonard. He will need all the skills he has learned from the Indians, as well as great courage and determination, if he is to succeed. But what will happen to the young woman if they do reach safety? And will he ever be able to return to his own people?

AT SENECA CASTLE
Illustrated by G. A. Harker

In this sequel to *The White Seneca*, Henry Cochrane, now eighteen, faces many perils as he serves as a scout for the Continental Army. General Washington is determined to do whatever it takes to stop the constant Indian attacks on the settlers and yet Henry is torn between his love for the Senecas and his loyalty to his own people. As the Army advances across New York State, Henry receives permission to travel ahead and warn his Indian friends of the coming destruction. But will he reach them in time? And what has happened to the beautiful Constance Leonard whom he had been forced to leave in captivity a year earlier?

THE SIGN ABOVE THE DOOR

Young Prince Martiesen is ruler of the land of Goshen in Egypt, where the Hebrews live. Eight plagues have already come upon Egypt and now Martiesen has been forced by Pharaoh to further increase the burden of the Hebrews. Martiesen, however, is in love with the beautiful Hebrew maiden, Elisheba, whom he is forbidden by Egyptian law to marry. As the nation despairs, the other nobles turn to Martiesen for leadership, but before he can decide what to do, Elisheba is kidnapped by the evil Peshala and terrifying darkness falls over the land. An exciting tale woven around the events of the Exodus from the Egyptian perspective!

www.SalemRidgePress.com

Adventure by George Manville Fenn

YUSSUF THE GUIDE
Being the Strange Story of the Travels in Asia Minor of
Burne the Lawyer, Preston the Professor, and
Lawrence the Sick
Illustrated by John Schönberg

Young Lawrence, an invalid, convinces his guardians, Preston the Professor and Burne the Lawyer, to take him along on an archaeological expedition to Turkey. Before they set out, they engage Yussuf as their guide. Through the months that follow, the friends travel deeper and deeper into the remote regions of central Turkey on their trusty horses in search of ancient ruins. Yussuf proves his worth time and time again as they face dangers from a murderous ship captain, poisonous snakes, sheer precipices, bands of robbers and more. Memorable characters, humor and adventure abound in this exciting story!

www.SalemRidgePress.com